OVEN BAKED
SECRETS

Eugeena Patterson Mystery, Book 2

Tyora Moody

Tymm Publishing LLC
Columbia, SC

Oven Baked Secrets
A Eugeena Patterson Mystery, Book 2

Copyright © 2015 by Tyora Moody

Oven Baked Secrets is a work of fiction. Names, characters, places and incidents either are products of the author's imagination or are used fictitiously. Any resemblance to actual persons, living or dead, events, or locales is entirely coincidental.

Published by Tymm Publishing LLC
701 Gervais Street, Suite 150-185
Columbia, SC 29201
www.tymmpublishing.com

Cover Design: TywebbinCreations.com
Cover Illustration: CinnamonSaturday.com
Editing: TheJStandard.com

Chapter 1

A subtle but distinct scent entered my nostrils as I walked through the front door of Hillcrest Manor Nursing Home. I first noticed this peculiar whiff of air last week. The scent reminded me of mothballs and my past adventures in antique stores. It always struck me that the beautifully crafted furniture used to belong to someone who was gone and possibly even forgotten. It never failed. Immediately after that smell smacked my nose, my next thought was how people could be carefully tucked away in a place like this and in some cases, forgotten.

I'm not sure if the nursing home was trying some new air freshener or if I was becoming more sensitive about my approaching sixtieth birthday, more so than I thought I would. I mean, what if I ended up in a place like this one day?

Not. I, Eugeena Patterson, would put up a real good fight with somebody before they tucked me away in some nursing home. I imagined I didn't have anything to worry about anytime soon, but I still told my three adult children if they tried to put me in a home before I was ready, I'd whip 'em first.

Even though it took me some time to adjust, I was now enjoying my retirement and my empty nest. I mean really, when I think over my life and all that I've been through, like the old folks say, "It's a wonder how I got over."

I headed to the front desk to check in as a visitor. I missed the busybody of our neighborhood. Not much went past those sharp blue eyes. At seventy years old, Louise Hopkins was hands down my oldest friend in the world. She was also officially my very first white best friend. Funny thing was we didn't too much like each other at first, but God surprised us both. We have gossiped and shared some good laughs, not to exclude raising our children and burying our husbands. It's amazing how time had flown in thirty years.

About five months ago, Louise's nosiness led to an attack in her home. After a major bump on the head, she hadn't been quite right, but bless her heart she was trying to get back to her old self. Then that son of hers got the bright idea he knew what was best. Sugar Creek hasn't been quite the same since the day I watched Louise's only child, William, move his mother out of her home.

I didn't agree with William's timing at all because I do believe Louise would've been just fine after some time in rehab. Being retired, it wouldn't have been much trouble at all for me to check on my dear friend from time to time.

I approached the front desk, putting on my best smile. "Hey honey, I'm here to see Louise Hopkins."

A petite woman who I hadn't seen before looked up at me and raised her eyebrow as though she didn't believe me. "I didn't know Mrs. Hopkins had visitors." She started pecking on the keyboard and frowned at the monitor in front of her.

I tried to peer to the side to view the monitor a bit better. She stopped typing and looked at me. "Excuse me, ma'am. One moment please."

I stepped back as if I had been scolded. I stared at the young woman wondering how she managed to get this job. Her blond hair was cut into a pixie style and rested flat against her head except for a small tuft in the front that appeared to have been colored pink at one time. Only the ends were pinkish. I read her name plate.

"Lexi, you must be new? I visit with Louise on Sundays after church. My name should be in your computer records."

Lexi sighed, "I'm sorry. We just installed this new system last week and I just don't see your name. I will need you to fill out some paperwork and I will print you a badge."

"Okay." I started to say something else, but remembered I was still wearing my church clothes. It probably wasn't wise to be looking like a hypocrite on Sunday. Not that any day of the week was a good time to lay your Christian principles down. I knew a new director had been hired recently at the nursing home and security had become a priority. I guess that was a good thing.

The world was full of crazy folks!

Lexi handed me a clipboard. As I reached for it, I noticed the many fields on the form. *What is this? A criminal background screening?*

A nurse came up behind the desk and grabbed the clipboard out of my hand.

Thank goodness. The cavalry had arrived. Patricia Brown known as Pat to me was a member of my church,

Missionary Baptist. I knew her mother and aunt very well and had watched Pat grow up alongside my sons.

She was eyeing the young woman. "Girl, you need to stop with this nonsense."

Lexi glared at Pat. "This is against protocol. Mrs. Saunders will not be pleased."

"I *know* Ms. Eugeena. Everyone around here knows her." Pat shook her head and adjusted her shoulder-length curly wig. I could count on Pat to wear a different wig each week. "Hey, Ms. Eugeena. It's so good to see you. Really, you don't have to fill all that out."

"Thank you, Pat. I do appreciate you. It's nice to have some folks used to seeing my face around here." I gave Lexi the side-eye look. "Besides, I know I have to be in the computer already."

Lexi looked at both Pat and me like we should be sent to detention. Lucky for us the phone rang diverting her attention from us.

Pat walked around the desk and grabbed my arm. She grinned wide, showing off the gap between her front teeth. "The new girl is a bit much. She's been aggravating people all week."

"I see. I can understand wanting to do well on your new job."

"I guess you're right. Anyway it is so good that Miss Louise has such a wonderful friend like you, Ms. Eugeena. You and her son are the only ones who come to visit her. Of course, *William* hasn't been by to see his mother in about a month."

I knew it! That boy just tucked his mama in a nursing home so he didn't have to be bothered with her. "Have you called him?"

Pat frowned as we walked down the hallway. "I've tried

to call him a few times. Especially the past two weeks since Mrs. Hopkins has been having trouble sleeping. She says she's having bad dreams, and she gets real agitated."

I wasn't surprised. I had decided either Louise was the nosiest woman I'd ever met or in a past life my sister friend had learned some super spy skills. She always knew what was going on in Sugar Creek before most people realized it. I later learned that Louise suffered from insomnia. The woman never slept.

Pat continued her report. "Yeah, she was so frustrated. Poor thing. We have her on some medicine to help her rest, so she may be a little woozy." Pat stopped walking, looked around and lowered her voice. "If you see Miss Louise's son, please tell him it's really important he comes to see me?"

I frowned. I don't think I've seen Pat quite so serious. "Is something going on?"

Pat glanced around again. "You will see what I'm talking about. Be sure William talks to me."

"I sure will." As I watched Pat go into another patient's room, I tried to think positive thoughts because Louise would ask what I was frowning about and I certainly didn't want to say, "Your son." I wasn't sure when I would see William.

I just found out last week he decided to put Louise's house on the market. I only knew that because I went out to the mailbox and noticed a for sale sign in the front yard. *Really!*

Louise was simply *not* replaceable as a neighbor.

As I continued to Louise's room I passed by a sitting area, I noticed an old black and white movie was playing on the television. The residents sitting around the television didn't appear to be moved by the action on the small screen. I hurried down the hallway. Getting old was depressing me more than I wanted to admit.

I paused for a minute before entering Louise's room. Last week I had noticed Louise's pretty blue eyes had a dullness that was disheartening.

I took a deep breath and smiled as I entered the room. Louise's room was the brightest room on the hall, painted in a banana yellow, to resemble her home. Her son did have sense enough to use his mother's money wisely and pay for a private room.

The afternoon sun shone through the window casting a glare across the television screen so I couldn't tell what Louise was watching. As I turned towards Louise, I stopped in my tracks and frowned. A young woman was standing on one side of Louise's bed peering intently down at her sleeping face. My first thought was maybe the young woman was a nurse, but she was definitely not wearing scrubs. I couldn't tell if she was wearing a bright pink shirt or a dress over what appeared to be striped leggings.

She seemed older than my youngest child, Leesa, who had recently turned twenty-two. I didn't think she was near the age of my sons, late thirties to early forties. I guessed she was between twenty-five and thirty.

My first thought was something certainly wasn't right about the woman being in Louise's room. Did she have to go through security out there at the front desk, and if so, who was she? Perhaps she was a volunteer. Whoever she was she hadn't noticed I'd walked in the room. I cleared my throat. "Honey, do you work here?"

The woman jumped backwards away from Louise like she'd been caught doing something she had no business. Her honey-colored skin appeared flushed. A colorful scarf was wrapped around her naturally curly hair, pushing it to the top of her head like a crown. She reminded me of one of the singers my daughter liked, Alicia Keys.

For some reason the woman kept walking backwards, and she bumped into the small table behind her. She stopped as if to steady herself and stuttered, "No, I don't work here."

This woman was acting way too nervous for me. Louise had ended up in a nursing home due to being attacked by a young person she and I had befriended this past summer. I couldn't go through this again. I moved into the room, closer to Louise's bed. "Then what are you doing here in this room? Are you looking for somebody?"

The strange young woman looked over at Louise and then back at me. She bit her lip and tugged on her hands behind her back like my five year old granddaughter. Using my teacher voice, the one I had once used for seventh graders when they'd were trying to be grown in my classroom, I commanded, "Miss, you better explain yourself and do it fast. I'm going to have to call security on you."

She pulled her hands from behind her back and waved them in front of her. "No, no don't do that. I don't mean any harm. I just wanted to see her."

"Louise Hopkins? You wanted to see her?" I pointed towards Louise who seemed to be knocked out to the world, oblivious to the conversation between me and the young woman. "Why?"

I could hear that woman's gulp clear across the room before she finally stammered out. "I wanted to meet my grandmother."

Uh, yeah right? The Louise Hopkins I had known all

these years didn't have any grandchildren. Who did this child think she was fooling?

Chapter 2

I blinked. I opened my mouth and then shut it to give my mind a chance to process. I stared at the girl. Despite her creative outfit, she was really a pretty little thing, her big eyes were slanted and she had full lips that would've rivaled Angelina Jolie's. I guess what I was seeking was some resemblance. It occurred to me despite my rash response, that the girl could've been telling the truth.

Louise's son, William, wasn't exactly the most responsible man in the world despite him being well over forty years old. He'd never married, but it's quite possible he had a love child. How often had I heard Louise talk about wanting to be a grandmother? Why would William keep that from his mother? Or did William know he was a father?

I motioned for the girl to walk away from the side of Louise's bed. As she came closer, I placed my hand on my hip. "Are you trying to tell me you're Louise's grand-daughter?"

The woman shook her head like she had a puppet master pulling her strings. "Yes, ma'am."

I looked at her for a minute and then shook my head as if this was a bad dream. Despite my better judgment, I said exactly what came to my mind. It just slipped out. "No sugar, that can't be."

The girl stepped back as if offended. "Ma'am?"

"You see I've known Louise for many, many years. If this woman had a grandchild she would've told the whole world."

The girl put her hand on her hip. "I told you I'm her granddaughter. My mom told me so and she wouldn't lie about it."

I held my hand up as if stopping traffic. "Okay, calm down. Let's start over. I don't think I introduced myself. I'm Eugeena Patterson, Louise's next door neighbor. Now tell me your name?"

The girl let out a sigh before responding. "I'm Jocelyn Miller."

"That's a pretty name. So, you live around here?" I hated small talk, but I was really digging for more information. What I did know was William didn't stay put for long and he'd only recently been back in South Carolina the last few months.

"I was raised in Beaufort."

"Oh. Gullah country." The language from West Africa still thrived in certain areas of South Carolina and mixed with English it was known as Gullah.

Jocelyn smiled. "Yes, I have relatives that talk Gullah or Geechee."

I glanced over at Louise, wondering if she could hear us. Was she just pretending to be sleep or had that medicine really knocked her out? I wanted to shake her awake. Jocelyn seemed like a nice woman, but I still wasn't sure what was going on.

I cleared my throat. "Jocelyn, did your mother tell you about your father? I mean have you met him?"

She frowned. "What do you mean?"

"Your dad is Miss Louise's son." Knowing his egotistical behind, William might have known about his daughter and rejected the girl. That would have been a real shame.

Jocelyn started to shake her head furiously. "My dad's name is David Miller."

Words escaped me. And my head started to hurt because this girl was confusing the mess out of me. "Is David your dad or your step-dad?"

"My biological dad."

I'm a smart, educated woman, with three grown children, four grandchildren and one on the way. Children aren't this complicated. Okay some of us do come in the world a bit willy-nilly, me being one of those people. But this girl can't be related to Louise as much as she would like to be. "Honey, I'm trying to work with you here. Are you sure you have the right room?"

"Mrs. Patterson, I promise you; I have the right room. This woman is my grandmother. Look, I will show you something and you tell me what you see." Jocelyn went over to the chair in the corner.

I hadn't noticed the hot pink backpack. I watched her pull out a black marbled notebook. She flipped it open and pulled out what appeared to be a photo. Jocelyn walked around the bed and handed it to me. "Here, this is my family. I'm much younger on this one, only about sixteen. There's my mom, dad and my brother. My dad passed away a few years ago."

I took the photo from her. Now I could tell this girl was telling the truth about her father. Despite the difference in skin tones, Jocelyn was the spitting image of the dark brown-skinned man. Jocelyn definitely had his eyes.

Now Jocelyn shared the same honey-colored complexion as her mom. Both mom and daughter shared the same full lips.

That's when it hit me.

The more and more I stared at Jocelyn's mom, I started to see something. It was the heart shape of the woman's face and her eyes. The woman's complexion was more bronze, but her eyes were vivid blue. I glanced at Jocelyn, who was staring back at me with bated breath.

Then I looked back at the photo.

Dear Lord!

Louise moaned from the bed. I stared over in her direction catching as my friend's eyes flickered open.

Louise Hopkins, you got some explaining to do.

There was no denying this one. In a lifetime I didn't know anything about, had my dear old friend given birth to a daughter? It didn't go past me that the woman in the photo was mixed race. So who could have been the father of Louise's love child?

Chapter 3

I handed the photo back to Jocelyn. I couldn't look at the young woman because my eyes were fixated on Louise. Her luminous blue eyes blinked as she continued to wake up from her slumber. I was nervous, almost scared nervous. Things were different now and the old Louise wasn't totally there. The viciousness of her attack a few months ago, crossing over into her seventies, and losing her independence had taken a cruel bite.

What should I do? Should I make this woman leave the room?

From my side view, I could see Jocelyn standing with her hands stuffed in her pockets. She'd noticed Louise was awake now. "Maybe she'll give us answers now." The girl looked at me hopefully.

My visit to the nursing home today was turning out to be crazier than an episode of *Days of Our Lives*. Mainly because somebody I knew, or didn't know as well as I thought, had been *Young and Restless*. I wasn't here in judgment because I had my firstborn at age seventeen. That was something that Louise knew about me.

"Eugeena." Louise blinked at me and rubbed her eyes. Her eyes were watery from being knocked out so long. "It sure is good to see you my friend."

I went to the side of the bed and patted her hand. "You too, Louise."

Louise grinned and asked, "How are you and Amos doing?"

Only Louise would wake up trying to be nosey about someone's love life. Not that me and Amos Jones were being romantic or anything like that.

I crossed my arms. "Louise, there you go starting something. I told you, Amos and I are just friends." I did like cooking for Amos though. In fact, tonight was one of our supper nights. It was better than both of us eating alone. I'm the first to admit I was pleasantly surprised how nice if was to have companionship, but he certainly was not my boyfriend. That stuff is for young folks.

I concentrated back on Louise's face. "Where do you get all these ideas? You know I'm too old."

"Eugeena, you are never too old for love." Louise raised her head up and looked around the room. Her eyes focused on Jocelyn. The young woman had been standing, listening to our conversation. I'd almost forgotten she was there.

It struck me funny that all Louise had to do was mention Amos to me and my mind went in a whole new direction.

Louise smiled. "Honey, you are such a pretty girl. Isn't she, Eugeena?"

I glanced at Jocelyn. "Yes, she is." I wasn't so sure if Jocelyn should be there. I had a growing suspicion in my gut. Jocelyn might have been sincere in her quest, but why now?

"Well, child, what can I do for you?" Louise coughed and tried to sit up.

I helped Louise get her pillows positioned behind her back. "Louise, maybe we should get Pat or one of the other nurses in here to check on you. You've been sleeping for a while."

Louise waved her hand. "No, I'm fine."

"Are you sure?" I really didn't want the unexpected family reunion to happen, although in the back of my mind I sure wanted to know if Louise really had a long lost daughter.

Jocelyn walked closer to the bed.

I eyed her. I had no intentions of moving from Louise's side.

Jocelyn glanced at me and then at Louise. "I have something to give you." She extended her hand with the photo I had just seen towards Louise.

Louise asked, "What is it, child? You got the saddest eyes."

"No." I protested before I knew I was going to object. I didn't feel right about this. Now wasn't the time. Louise had made so much progress after getting bumped on the head this past summer.

Louise held out her right hand. She was studying Jocelyn's face and maybe she saw something. I could see that similar heart-shaped feature in Jocelyn's face now too.

My friend took the photo into her trembling hands. I looked around for the nurse's buzzer. I certainly hoped I didn't have to use it, but I wasn't sure what was about to happen.

Louise stared at the photo for the longest time. I'm not used to that much silence from her, so I touched my friend's shoulder. "Louise, are you okay?"

She just kept staring at the photo.

I looked over at Jocelyn. The poor woman had tears streaming down her face. She was doing one of those ugly cries, the kind where your face scrunches up in hope of pushing the tears back. It wasn't working, but she still managed to look cute.

Right then, my nose started to run. That wasn't a good sign for me. That meant my emotions were bubbling to the surface and my nose was the exit. The seriousness of this situation had officially shaken me up. There was no turning back.

I patted Louise's left hand. "Louise, are you okay? Do I have to get a nurse for you?"

Louise whispered a response.

"What?" I leaned down. I thought I heard her say no, but her voice was hoarse and low. I watched as tears spilled down into the wrinkles on Louise's face.

Lord Jesus, this is worse than a soap opera. I've been dropped into a Lifetime movie.

I grabbed several tissues from the table next to Louise's bed. I shuffled over and pushed some into Jocelyn's hands. I went to Louise and stuffed tissues in her free hand.

The tissue I had left in my hand I used to blow my own nose. While I honked my nose, I could hear voices approaching down the hallway. *Probably some of the residents.*

A man's voice exploded in anger as the voices approached closer to Louise's room. Jocelyn wiped her face and turned to the door, looking confused. Louise stopped staring at the photo and turned her head towards the door.

That's when I realized who was currently standing out in the hallway, and who I suspected was arguing with Pat about Louise. At that very moment, I also knew Jocelyn needed to leave and this conversation needed to happen some other time.

But before I could encourage Jocelyn to exit the room, William Hopkins entered the room. All six foot two of him seemed to take up the doorway, blocking the way of escape.

Chapter 4

Poor Louise. I turned towards her and I noticed the hand that held the photo had gone limp. Louise's eyes were closed. Was she faking like she just fainted or did her son's sudden arrival knock her flat? Whatever just happened, my friend was going down fast. Before I addressed William and Pat, I reached over and snatched the photo out of Louise's hand. Her only son certainly didn't need to see it right then. I slipped the photo into my dress pocket as I turned to face William.

"Pat, I think you need to check on Louise. She woke up, but she doesn't appear to be feeling well."

"Oh my." Pat gave William a withering look and pointed to Louise. "I told you she has not been doing well." Pat rushed over to Louise's side.

I stepped away from the bed to move out of Pat's way and to examine William a little more closely. From the look of William's face, he appeared flushed with anger from his conversation with Pat. Despite being a nurse, Pat had a good heart and didn't mind speaking her mind about her patients.

I didn't too much care for William's hurt male pride, but I had a very distinct feeling he was up to something because his appearance was past odd to me. This was a man who most of his life didn't have a problem looking unkempt. His usually wore his hair pulled back into a ratty long ponytail. Lord knows, he always managed to look like he needed a bath.

I looked William up and down from head to toe. I don't know who knocked some sense into William and gave him a makeover, but it was long overdue. The man actually had a real haircut that showed off his graying temples. He was no George Clooney, but he actually resembled a distinguished middle-aged man. What was even more shocking was he was wearing a suit which I gathered was not cheap.

Now it was Sunday, but the last I heard William was very much against any kind of religious establishment, and was borderline atheist to the chagrin of his mother.

I crossed my arms. "William, Pat was just telling me they haven't seen you in a while. I'm so glad to see you here today."

William glared at me and then Jocelyn before responding. "I've been pretty busy. I just came by today to let my mother know I found a potential buyer for the house." He frowned at me. "Mrs. Patterson, I told you, you don't have to go out of your way to visit my mother."

I about choked out a retort. *I did not need a new neighbor and how dare you be that thoughtless.* But there was a pretty volatile secret in the room, so I said a prayer to keep my thoughts to myself and responded as sweet as I could. "William, you know your mother and I have been friends a long time. I'm always going to be available when Louise needs me. You're looking mighty spiffy today. Did you make it to church?"

William grimaced. "I'm trying something a little different. Anyway if you're finished visiting, I really need to talk to my mother."

I watched as William's eyes refocused like a slot machine as he looked in Jocelyn's direction.

He inquired, "And who are you?"

I grabbed Jocelyn's arm. This was not the time to be spouting the granddaughter claim. "Jocelyn and I were just leaving. We have a lot of catching up to do."

Louise let out a moan that made me want to jump out of my skin. Yes indeed, there could be some catastrophic consequences in the room. William was an only child for as long as I had known. He wouldn't be accepting of another sibling or any family coming out the woodwork at this point in his life.

I wouldn't be surprised if he wasn't waiting for Louise to die and pass along all that money her husband had left her. Even before she married, Louise had already inherited family money and was quite the catch from younger photos I had seen. Louise had always led a simple life, but her roots in Charleston could be traced back to a plantation.

Jocelyn pulled her arm out of my grip and grabbed her backpack. "You're right, Mrs. Patterson. I need to go."

Under the circumstances, I'm glad she agreed.

William narrowed his eyes and stepped towards Jocelyn. "I've seen you some place, haven't I?"

Jocelyn slid a look at me and shook her head vehemently. "I doubt it. I really need to go." Jocelyn sprinted from the room like someone was chasing her.

"Jocelyn." I moved as fast as I could to the door, but she was halfway down the hallway by the time I stepped out of the room. I didn't want her to leave like that. Besides I wanted to know why she showed up now.

Why did William think he'd seen her before? I would catch up with him later.

I moved down the hallway fast, thankful that most of the weight I've been trying to lose this year had been sliding off steadily. I caught up to Jocelyn just as she was about to get into her car. Her bright red Honda Civic was parked right next to my Toyota Camry. I made my body move faster and reached Jocelyn's as she turned on the car's ignition. I banged on the window on the driver's side.

She looked at me like the crazy woman I probably appeared to be.

I shouted, "Can you please open the door? This isn't over yet."

Jocelyn rolled the window down and stared at me.

I was really too old to be chasing someone down. I gulped as I tried to catch my breath. "Look, I believe you are sincere in your efforts and I want to help."

Jocelyn shook head and then stated, "Don't worry about it."

"What? Did you not come here for answers?"

Jocelyn gripped the steering wheel as if she wanted to tear it off. "This was a mistake. My mom didn't even know I was doing this. When she told me about her past, she told me that she'd let it go. That it wasn't worth knowing. I see what my mom was trying to tell me now."

I shook my head. I was really trying to understand, but was starting to feel a bit faint myself. It was past time for me to get some food in my system and today's visit had been a bit too exciting. "Look, honey, that woman in there is one of my best friends. I know when she looked at the photo, she saw something. She was a little emotional, but

I think she wanted to connect with you. Why don't you give me a few days and maybe I can make it happen."

Jocelyn sighed and looked over at me. "You're really kind, Mrs. Patterson. I'm glad we met today, but please don't worry. I can tell you there are some things from the past that shouldn't be stirred up. Like I said, I should've listened to my mom." With that Jocelyn pressed the button to raise up the window and placed the car in reverse.

I stepped away as she started to back out into the parking lot. It was really a shame that Jocelyn wanted to give up because my curiosity had just kicked in. I'd seen regret in Louise's eyes a while ago. Losing one of my other best friends a few months back taught me a thing or two about regrets and dealing with the past.

I walked around to my car's driver's side, unlocked the door and climbed in. Before I started the car, I reached into my purse and pulled out some crackers. The crackers would last me until I got a real meal. I munched and digested all that I had heard and seen in the last hour.

When I finished, I dusted the crumbs from my dress and reached to bring the seatbelt around my hips. I felt something in my pocket. I pulled out the photo that I had grabbed from Louise's hands before her son entered the room. I looked closely at the woman who was Jocelyn's mother.

She had to be Louise's daughter.

Jocelyn said she was around sixteen in this picture. Seeing Jocelyn today, I would guess the photo was ten years old. Jocelyn's mother was probably about a decade behind me. She shared the same heart-shaped face as Louise, but the bridge of her nose was a bit wider and her lips were full. *Who was the father?*

Louise was married briefly before she married

William's father, William Hopkins, Sr., better known to most people as Bill. She didn't talk much about her first marriage, but I knew she'd lost a baby and a not too long after that her first husband asked for a divorce and ran off with another woman. I assumed Louise gave this baby up for adoption before she married the first husband.

How is it that all these years Louise never thought to confide in me? Oh yeah, I was preparing to stir up whatever I could from the past.

Chapter 5

Jocelyn Miller and her family haunted me all the way home. I felt compelled to see her again. I did have a photo she may want returned. Plus, there were too many questions left unanswered. I consider myself a pretty transparent person. I have shared more details of my life with Louise than I would like to admit, but that's what friends do, they share their lives. I could imagine the circumstances around the birth of this child led Louise down a road where talking about the situation didn't help.

Did it ever occur to Louise that her child or in this case, the grandchild, would come looking for her? Why was Jocelyn doing the search instead of her mother?

I knew just the person who could help me find her too. If there was some way I could get back in touch with Jocelyn, Amos Jones was my man.

My man for getting to the bottom of a situation. Not my man.

I'd been married thirty-seven years and widowed five years. I'm just not interested in going back to being in a romantic relationship. Now I would love to see my two youngest children, Cedric and Leesa married. But me, I'm fine. Been there, done that as they say. Sometimes I felt like I spent way too much time trying to convince myself.

I drove my car down Sugar Creek with the intentions of starting on the Sunday dinner I'd planned for Amos and me. I couldn't wait to show him the photo, quiz him about Jocelyn and get his take on my suspicions. I did like to hear that man talk. Kind of like my Ralph, he wasn't full on words, but when he did talk, he had plenty to say.

I guess most men are like that, only choosing to say what's most important. Women tended to chit chat and be all over the place in a conversation.

When I pulled up to the front of my home, to my surprise there was a very familiar aqua blue car in the driveway. I don't know why I would be surprised. My one and only daughter showed up at random.

I parked beside my daughter's car and looked over to my right to see Leesa and her children on my porch. I love seeing my grandchildren, but was feeling suspicious about the Sunday visit. I babysat last week and there was no mention of a need for my free services. Leesa was known to drop off her kids and take off. A few months ago when she did this, I had no idea where she had gone and was worried sick enough to report her missing. Since that incident Leesa had moved to Charleston. I watched my grandchildren on occasion at an agreed upon time because while I was retired, a woman liked her freedom.

Besides I wasn't that lonely anymore with my empty nest. After my friend Mary was killed this past summer, I inherited her spoiled Corgi. That little dog was like another child, just with four legs.

I climbed out the car and headed towards my porch.

Kisha came running down the steps. "Grandma, we came to visit you."

For just a few hours, I hope. I held out my arms to my one and only granddaughter. My other grandchildren were boys. Girls seemed a dime a dozen in my family. It was just Ralph and the two boys for the longest time until I had Leesa at age thirty-eight. It certainly helped to mix up the testosterone monopoly with some estrogen. "How's my girl doing?" I squeezed Kisha and then placed my hands on her small shoulders. "My, my I believe you've grown since the last time I saw you."

Kisha jumped up and down. "Mama, let me mark my height on the kitchen door." She stopped jumping and held her hand up next to the top of her head. "I grew this much."

"You're going to be tall as your mama and grandmamma soon." I glanced over at my other grandchild, Tyric, who was now sitting up grinning. Almost six months old, Leesa's son was a bundle of joy too. As I walked up the porch steps, I looked my daughter up and down to make sure we had some type of understanding. "Well, it's good to see you. I'm about to make dinner."

Leesa grinned. "I know. We were hoping to join you."

I shook my head. I was just planning dinner for Amos and me, but I usually fixed extra because I never knew when my man child, Dr. Cedric Patterson, would stop by. Lately, now that he and his girlfriend, Carmen, were shacking, I didn't see him as much. Cedric knew to stay away from me because I had some choice words to say about a man so close to forty not marrying a woman. Really, I thought I raised that boy better than that.

As I opened the door, my housemate came running and barking. My dearly departed husband, Ralph Patterson, would have never allowed any animal in the house. My little furry friend gave me some normalcy. While Kisha and Porgy went off to play, I changed out of my church clothes into a warm velour outfit that was suitable for comfort and entertaining guests.

I had laid the photo that I had acquired from the young woman on my dresser. Jocelyn's comment about not stirring up the past still bothered me. *Why did the young woman feel compelled to see Louise today? Why wouldn't she let her mother know?* Maybe Louise's long lost daughter had also tried to reach out to Louise but with unfavorable results.

I placed the photo in my trouser pocket and tried to put my thoughts on hold. I had a Sunday meal to pull together in a few hours. The past and all of its secrets weren't going anywhere.

I went downstairs and stepped into the kitchen. I already had some chicken thawing in the fridge. I did a lot of oven baked recipes since the fall weather had arrived. Something about a toasty kitchen from the oven made the house cozy and reminiscent of the days when it was full of family. Plus, it didn't hurt to use the oven with my new healthier eating habits.

As I seasoned the chicken, I looked over at Leesa who was bouncing Tyric on her knee. A few months back she hadn't adjusted too well to the newborn. Part of the reason for her moving closer to me was so she could go see a therapist about her postpartum depression. As a teenager, Leesa suffered from depression, and I had always felt I should have been more vigilant about seeking help for her. Sometimes you need to place pride to the side and do what is best for a loved one's mental state.

I covered the chicken with aluminum foil and placed the glass pan inside the oven. I pulled out a chair at the table and sat down to finish chopping up the vegetables. Since I've been retired, I've started to use social media a bit more. I loved using Pinterest to find lesson plans and activities my last few years in the classroom, but lately I've been pinning oven baked or roasted recipes. *The Wednesday Chef* had a great recipe for roasted vegetables that I have tried at least three times. I can't say I was ever into zucchini and eggplant before, but I like them alongside the carrots and potatoes. Instead of onions I decided to substitute one of my favorite vegetables, squash.

While I chopped, I thought it was a good time to check on my daughter's on and off again boyfriend. Chris Black was Tyric's father. On my first meeting with Chris the large, intimidating man and police officer didn't meet my approval at all. When Kisha mentioned Chris had hit her, I had questions about the man's temperament and if he was really a good fit to be around my daughter and her children. I have seen him several times since our first meeting. He seemed to be trying. "Has Chris come down to visit you and the children lately?"

Leesa smiled. "Chris came to visit yesterday and we took the kids to the South Carolina Aquarium."

"Oh well, that was nice. Sounds like you two are acting like a family."

Leesa eyed me. "We working through some things, but Chris does love me and the kids."

I wasn't encouraging Leesa to do any more than make sure Chris was a part of his son's life. I didn't like when a man was irresponsible. I wasn't one to encourage a woman to marry a man if there were signs of immaturity. Marriage is simply not taken seriously these days. Divorce is too easy and quick to choose. I responded. "I just want to see you happy and married to the *right* man for you and the children." I stood from the chair and grabbed the pan for the vegetables.

"Well, what about you, Mama?"

I looked at Leesa. I knew what she was trying to ask me, but ignored her until I mixed all the vegetables into the pan. I placed the pan down and gave my attention back to my daughter's face. "What? What about me?"

Leesa raised her eyebrow. "You sure me and the kids aren't interfering with your Sunday dinner with Mr. Amos?"

"Who said I was cooking just for Amos? I have to eat too." I covered the vegetables and turned my back to check on the chicken. I thought I was the mother and interrogating was my job.

Leesa laughed. "I'm just teasing you, Mama, but Cedric said we should give you some time with Amos."

I shook my head and then reached for the pan of vegetables. "Your brother needs to tend to his own business. I still don't see why he asked Carmen to move in with him. What happened to proposing, getting engaged, married and then move in together?" I placed the pan of vegetables on the rack above the chicken.

Leesa responded. "Geez, Mama! People like to do a trial period. I mean most marriages don't work out. You and dad were rare."

I closed the oven door a bit too hard and placed my hand on my hip. "Because we decided to stick it out and work through our issues." I didn't understand the world, but then again God gave us all free will. It was up to us to make our own choices. "Let me hold Tyric while we wait on the food to finish cooking."

Leesa handed my grandson to me. "My, my you're getting to be a big fellow already." The men in our family and

Tyric's dad were well over six feet so I imagined my grandson would be a giant too. As I bounced him on my knee, my mind wandered back to Louise.

My friend had a baby many, many years ago. I wondered how often she had thought about that child. Did Louise even know that she had a little girl? The child that Louise told me she miscarried had been a boy.

From the facial features of the woman in that photo, I suspected the father was a black man, which made me all the more curious. Louise was a teenager during the 1950s when interracial relationships were practically impossible. There was no way a black man was even supposed to look at a white woman. So how did my friend manage to have this secret love affair?

I decided I would pay another visit to my friend. The haunted look in Louise's eyes told me she longed for a child that she had lost for reasons far beyond her control.

Chapter 6

I enjoyed Amos' company not only because he was a great companion, but he enjoyed his food. As a cook most of my life, I liked to feed people and see them genuinely satisfied from the experience. Amos never disappointed.

I also liked that he didn't mind cleaning off the table. I have to say Amos and I had developed quite the Sunday tradition of eating dinner, cleaning up the dishes and then talking on the porch. We couldn't talk on the porch as much anymore because fall had finally arrived. Once the sun went down, the temperature and the sun dropped for the evening. So we moved the conversation to the living room. I was still looking forward to our conversation tonight since I had a lot to tell Amos.

I walked Leesa and the children to the car. Kisha held my hand extra tight like she didn't want to let go. No one would ever accuse me of having favorites, but this was my girl. My only granddaughter from my only daughter, us girls had to stick together. I let go of Kisha's hand and squeezed her until she giggled. Then I reached over and stole a kiss from Tyric. He giggled too. The smile on

Leesa's face warmed my heart. It was nice to see members of my family in a good place.

I pointed at Leesa. "Now you be sure to call me when y'all get home."

Leesa grinned. "Of course I will, Mama. You sure are in a hurry to get rid of us. I hope I don't have to tell my Mama to behave."

I swatted at my child. "Girl, get those children in the car."

After the Kisha and Tyric were buckled up safely in the backseat, Leesa winked at me and then climbed into the front seat. I waved as Leesa backed out of the driveway. With a sigh of relief, I turned and headed back into the house.

Before I opened the front door, I noticed another car coming down the street. I stood and watched the car turn into the driveway of Louise's house. It was William's car. He climbed out of the car and from what I could make out in the growing darkness William was still dressed in the suit. He stood and waited as another car arrived behind him.

Now who is that? I didn't know anything about cars, but it appeared the person was driving a sports car. I remembered that William said he'd found a buyer for the house. That meant I would have a new neighbor sooner than I thought. Driving a car like that made me a bit apprehensive. Why didn't William just move back home and let his mother live in peace in her own house? But that was my own selfishness, I guess.

I didn't want to appear too nosey so I moved farther inside the house, slightly closing the screen door. I wanted to see who would step out of the car. I heard the car door open, but it was kind of hard to see through the crack in the screen door.

I heard William say, "Hello. I'm so glad you could make it tonight. You're going to love the house."

"I can't wait to see it. It's just the way I remember it." The voice that responded in the darkness was female.

So there was a woman driving the car? Interesting. What did she mean by it's the way she remembered it?

It suddenly occurred to me with the lights on behind me that they would be able to see me. *That's not a good way to make a first impression, Eugeena.* Of course, intimidating my possible future neighbors sounded like a pretty good plan. Maybe the woman would decide not to buy the house since there was a crazy neighbor next door.

Knowing I had Amos waiting on me in the living room I closed the front door. I had to laugh because I had really taken on too many of Louise's habits. Now I was the neighborhood busybody. It was destined to happen. Long before I was head of neighborhood watch, Louise had that position and had pretty much helped established the watch. I still haven't figured out how the position was passed to me this year.

Amos peered at me as I entered the living room. "What's going on, Eugeena? You've been chomping at the bit all night."

I sat down with a huff in the chair opposite from Amos. He liked to sit in the recliner which used to belong to my deceased husband, Ralph. What was even stranger was how Porgy was sitting at Amos' feet. The Corgi looked over at me, but seemed to be content where he was lying. *My how life changes.*

I leaned against the back of the chair trying to figure out how to start my story. "I wanted to say something earlier, but neither Leesa nor the children needed to hear this story. It has quite a few twists and turns."

Amos raised his eyebrow. "Well, don't keep it to yourself any longer. What happened?"

He didn't have to encourage me anymore; I spilled the entire story of Jocelyn showing up at Louise's room, claiming to be her long lost granddaughter. I had slipped the photo from my pocket and pulled it out for him to view.

Amos studied the photo that I handed to him. When I mentioned William had showed up out of the blue, he shook his head. "Sounds like our neighbor has a bit of family drama stirring. Who knew?"

I shook my head. "I know! The thing that's really bothering me is there was a hint of longing in Louise's eyes like she knew this girl was related to her somehow. I just don't understand why Jocelyn changed her mind all of sudden."

"Well, Eugeena, if Jocelyn's own mother didn't come to search for Louise on her own, maybe the past needed to be left alone. Plus, it sounds like William made her nervous and it was best not to rock the boat."

I crossed my arms. "I agree William wouldn't have taken the news very well. He's over there now trying to sell the house. It just bothers me. Do you know how often I've heard Louise's desire to have grandchildren?"

"Yes, grandchildren from William."

I waved my hand. "That's not going to happen. William is just plain selfish and in his own world. You know it was really strange of him to show up all of sudden. He's up to something. The man was dressed up in a suit and looking like some businessman, which I doubt William has a single ounce of business sense."

What was that about anyway?

I sighed deeply. "Louise has barely been in that nursing

home a few months. That was her home for thirty years. He had no right."

Amos nodded. "I know she's been your neighbor and a really good friend, but all of us are getting older, Eugeena. Louise is his mother and his responsibility. I don't know if my daughters would even come to look after me."

I had sense enough to keep my mouth closed as Amos grew quiet. Amos was a good man, but he was caught up in his career as a police officer and then a detective while raising his children. Both of his daughters lived far away, one in California and the other one out in the Midwest somewhere. I knew Amos also longed to have contact with his own grandchildren.

A loud bang shook both of us from the quiet moment of reflection.

Porgy started barking and running in circles.

I stared over at Amos. "What was that—" Before I could finish my question, another loud noise sent both Amos and I from our seated positions.

"Get down." Amos hunched over. "That's definitely gunshots."

I whispered loudly, "Where are they coming from?"

Amos moved past me. "It sounds like it's coming from next door. Stay put."

Now that man knew better than to tell me to stay put. As Amos slowly opened the front door, I was right on his heels.

Amos hissed at me. "Woman, didn't I tell you to stay put. We don't know what's going on out here. Call 9-1-1."

"Okay, okay." I went to reach for the phone by the door, but noticed a car speeding away down the road. "Amos, that car was just in Louise's driveway. Can you see the license plate?"

Amos had already made his way outside and down the porch steps. At his age, I didn't know the man could still move that fast. Was that really the same car that drove up behind William's car a while ago? Surely the gunshots didn't come from next door. Maybe the woman was just scared off.

I was really concerned. I grabbed the cordless phone from the table in the hallway and dialed 9-1-1.

The dispatcher came on. "How can I help you?"

"I think there's been a shooting in my neighborhood."

"Can you tell us where you're located?"

"2045 Sugar Creek Drive." I hung up once I received confirmation that the police were on their way. I pushed open the screen door and peered into the darkness, but I didn't see a sign of Amos or anyone. "Amos?" I continued to grip the phone in my hand like it was a weapon and crept down the porch steps. I noticed William's car was still in the driveway, but the other car was gone now.

Did something happen to William?

I sure wish Amos would appear because I was really scared. I crept towards Louise's house. I knew if Amos saw me doing this, he would have some terse words about me staying put. Suppose he needed help? Amos had saved my life a few months before from walking into a situation that I should've thought through a bit better.

I stepped around William's car and noticed that the front door was wide open. I moved towards the door, hoping the police would arrive soon. As I drew closer, I peeked inside Louise's home, recognizing the layout of the living room. It was empty of all of Louise's furniture, belongings and cats. I had always wondered how William managed to gather all the cats. Louise had at least four or five in the house.

Amos was squatting down over a man's body on the floor. It took me a second before I realized it was William's body.

I swallowed and asked. "Amos, is William okay?"

Amos stood and looked at me. "Stay over there, Eugeena. This is a crime scene."

I had no intentions of walking anywhere near the scene. From what I could see from where I stood those bullets had landed in William's body. *But why?* I swallowed before I asked my next question, already knowing Amos' answer. "Does he need an ambulance?"

Amos shook his head. "He's gone, Eugeena."

As much as I didn't care for William, I wouldn't wish that kind of heartache on anyone. I had a feeling I would be the one to break my poor friend's heart about her beloved son and until recently was known to the world as her only living child.

Chapter 7

When the police finally arrived, I had to remind myself to listen to my phone messages. Sure enough Leesa had called while Amos and I were checking out the crime scene.

Leesa fussed, "You told me to call when we got home. You and Mr. Amos were that busy you couldn't come to the phone?"

"Girl, if you don't stop that foolishness. An emergency came up next door."

"What kind of emergency?"

"I can't get into it right now, Leesa. I'm glad you're home safe. Tell the children goodnight for me." After I hung up the phone it occurred to me that Leesa and the children had left only an hour before everything went down next door. That was too close for comfort.

It was cold, but Amos and I sat bundled up in our jackets on my porch. I didn't want to miss a single thing. Neither one of us were surprised when Detective Sarah Wilkes walked towards us. The red-haired detective had her long hair tied in a messy bun on the top of her head.

It wasn't that late, but Detective Wilkes looked like she lacked a few days sleep. She eyed me and then Amos before speaking. "Weren't you two the first ones on the scene of the last murder that happened in Sugar Creek?"

I was a bit offended by Detective Wilkes' tone, but Amos chuckled and responded. "Detective, Ms. Eugeena and I can't help that we have this much excitement around us. We're retired folks just trying to enjoy a Sunday evening."

Now I liked the way Amos set Missy straight. "Yes, it wasn't like we were expecting to hear two gunshots next door."

Detective Wilkes whipped out her notebook and pen. "You said you heard two gunshots. About what time?"

I don't know if Amos was paying attention to the clock or not. "Well, my daughter left around seven o'clock with my grandchildren and I think we'd been talking at least an hour. I would say around eight o'clock."

Amos nodded. "That sounds about right. The gunshots were coming from next door. I went out to check and saw the front door open."

I waved my hands. "We saw a car take off down the street. The car came up not long after William arrived."

Amos said, "Yes, a car sped off as I opened the door. It appeared to be a sports car. Maybe the latest Mustang. Dark in color, wouldn't you say, Eugeena?"

Now that Amos asked me I wasn't sure what I remembered. "It was dark outside. I would say it could have been black or dark gray. I'm not that sure."

Detective Wilkes continued, "That's fine. Did either of you happen to catch the license plate?"

Amos shook his head. "Nope. Whoever was in the car was moving fast."

I added, "I wasn't trying to be nosy, but I think it was a woman driving the car. I know I heard a female's voice." Now I wished I had stayed at the door being nosy. I might have been able to help William if I had seen the woman who showed up at his house.

Detective Wilkes scratched notes rapidly in her notebook. She tapped the pen and took a breath. "Okay. So, Mr. Jones you entered the crime scene?"

Amos lifted his chin. "I went to see if I could help Mr. Hopkins. When I saw his chest injuries, I reached over to check for a pulse." Amos paused. "I found none. I realized at that point that the scene needed to be protected for the Charleston CSU."

I shivered. I hadn't seen William's body up close, but Amos' description was enough for me. "I didn't enter the house, but I called 9-1-1."

Detective Wilkes shook her head and continued to scribble in her notebook. She looked up. "Did either of you notice anything strange other than the car? Isn't there an older woman that lives here too?"

I spoke up. "Louise is in a nursing home. William, the victim, placed her in a home in late July." It occurred to me that there was something I knew that could be helpful. "You know I did see William earlier today when I was visiting his mother. He mentioned that he found a buyer for the house. I believe the woman that was there tonight could have been the interested buyer."

Detective Wilkes nodded. "I will need the contact information for Mr. Hopkin's mother. Maybe she has more information on this buyer or buyers."

I nodded. "Sure, she's at Hillcrest Manor Nursing Home, but would you let me talk to her about her son. She's doesn't have any other family."

Now that was a fib, Eugeena. Louise certainly does have more family.

"Certainly, Mrs. Patterson. Why don't you get some sleep? We will touch base tomorrow morning."

After Detective Wilkes walked away, I turned to Amos. "I wasn't very truthful. Louise does have other family. Don't you think it's odd that this all happened today."

Amos eyed me. "Don't get any ideas, Eugeena. Like the detective said, let's get a good night's sleep and we'll talk more tomorrow. Lock your doors up tight."

"Okay." Amos stood on my porch until I shut my front door and locked it. Despite Amos' warning, I was full of questions.

Who was the woman that came to visit William? Was it really about a house sale or did William say that as a cover up for something else? Then there was that moment when William seemed suspicious of Jocelyn earlier. Did he know who she was?

I changed into my flannel nightgown and tried to settle my nerves, but so much had happened today I was too restless to just lie down. I knelt by my bedside and prayed for Louise and the loss of her son. *This is going to hit her hard, Lord.*

It occurred to me after I climbed into bed. What if today's visit from Jocelyn was a part of a plan that included taking out Louise's only heir?

Chapter 8

Dreams of Jocelyn shooting at William invaded my sleep. I don't know why because it seemed so illogical. While I couldn't clearly see the woman, I didn't think the female voice I heard was Jocelyn's voice. But then I kept replaying William's face as he questioned Jocelyn. Had he seen Jocelyn before? It was the timing of it all. There was so much more to my neighbor's son getting killed next door.

By the time I arose Monday morning I felt like I had run a race in my sleep. I lingered on my knees longer than usual in prayer because I didn't know how to tell Louise her son was dead. Louise's eyes had also haunted me as I slept. "How do I break the news to Louise gently, Lord. If it was one of my sons, I know I would need to be buckled down from the sheer pain."

I struggled up from my knees and turned to see my housemate watching me. I have to say Porgy impressed me more and more each day. Whenever I knelt down to pray, that little doggie of mine sat near me just as quiet as he could. I imagined when his former owner and my now deceased friend, Mary, prayed, the dog had gotten used to being quiet and almost reverent. No one could convince me animals were lacking sense.

"Alright, let's get going for the day." Porgy bounded down the steps before me. While he gobbled his Kibbles, I made a cup of green tea. Knowing I needed to eat, I made toast and then checked my glucose levels. I needed to remember to take care of me and my diabetes, which I must say has been quite a learning experience over the past year. Some days I still don't quite get it right.

After giving Porgy a good run in the backyard, I dressed and headed towards my car. I briefly looked over at Louise's house and found the yellow crime scene tape in the front of the house a bit sobering. All these years I've been here, I hadn't seen as much violent crime as I had in the past few months. Here was yet another death, this time right next door to me.

I felt a bit ashamed that I didn't even speak to William when he arrived yesterday, not that we were the kind of folks to greet each other. William had a distinct dislike for me and I never quite understood why when his mother and I were such good friends.

When Bill was alive, we all got along fine with him. Ralph and Bill would talk to each other across our yards. William and my boys grew up together. For whatever reason since he was a teenager, William had grown more distant and callous, even more so after his father died. Bill and William were always at odds. Louise would never admit it, but she and her beloved son were not that close either.

William stayed away for long periods of time telling Louise he was on some adventure somewhere. I had never really been clear on what William did for a living. I don't think Louise knew either. He struck me as a bit of a wanderer going from one scheme to another.

If only I had lingered outside long enough to catch his visitor up close. Would it have helped or would I have put me and Amos in danger?

What I really wished was that Amos or I had caught the license plate of that sports car that sped away. Though she was in the nursing home, Louise's mind was still active and she would ask questions about her son's death. I certainly had no answers. I was of no help and I didn't like that at all.

As I climbed into my car, I thought about asking Amos to tag along with me to the nursing home, but I knew the conversation ahead would become quickly emotional. Men didn't like to deal with a lot of emotions.

It took me all of ten minutes to arrive at the nursing home. I parked my car and sat for a moment to collect myself. I don't think I've ever done anything quite this hard. When my husband, Ralph, passed away, all the children were in town and by his side. We grieved together.

Louise would be grieving alone. It was time to face my friend.

When I stepped inside the nursing home I almost ran into a well-dressed woman. She wore a navy business suit and had a gold badge on the left side that read "director."

"Oh, sorry. I didn't mean to run you over."

"No problem, I shouldn't have been in a hurry." The woman pushed her glasses up to her face.

She had perfect flawless skin and brown eyes that blinked rapidly behind her silver wire frame glasses. I looked at her badge again. For some reason the woman reminded me more of a funeral director the way she held her hands in front of her. I'm sure that was my imagination running away with me again. The place just messed with my mind. "Are you the new director here?"

"Yes. I'm Jacqueline Saunders. Are you interested in taking a tour of our facilities?"

I shook my head. "Oh no I came to see a friend, Mrs. Hopkins; you may have heard she lost her son last night."

The director blinked. "Oh yes, it's very terrible news. We've been trying to keep that information from Mrs. Hopkins. It seems like you people are in a hurry to upset her."

"You people?" I asked.

Ms. Saunders turned her head. "There's a detective here."

I peeked around Ms. Saunders and saw Detective Wilkes standing at the desk area talking to the young woman that I had met yesterday. I hoped the detective hadn't seen Louise. I wanted to be there for support and to be the one to break the bad news to my friend.

"Oh my, well it's good to meet you, Ms. Saunders. I better see what's going on." I walked over to the desk. "Detective, I didn't know you would be here this soon."

Detective Wilkes turned towards me. Her red hair looked even more disheveled and her green eyes appeared to be dull. *Did this woman sleep?*

She answered, "Hello, Mrs. Patterson. I wanted to get in touch with Mrs. Louise Hopkins as soon as possible about her son's death."

"I'm glad I came early. She's going to be really upset. It was pretty much just William and her."

Detective Wilkes nodded. "I see. So, there's no other family?"

I thought to myself should I tell the detective about the young woman who was here yesterday. I really didn't get the impression that Jocelyn would do William any harm, but my dreams and suspicions last night weren't helping.

I answered the detective back the best I knew how. "Louise doesn't have other family that I know of. Her siblings were older and have passed on years ago."

Detective Wilkes looked at me as though she thought I would say something else. I glanced at Lexi who appeared to be busy behind the counter. She looked up from the computer screen to look at me and then the detective. That's when it occurred to me that Jocelyn may have mentioned she was Louise's granddaughter to get access to the room.

The detective shrugged. "Shall we go ahead and talk to Mrs. Hopkins?"

"Yes. I'm ready." No, I really wasn't, but the inevitable had to happen.

The detective and I walked down the hall in what felt like slow motion. There was no small talk between us. I twisted my hands as we drew closer to the door. I had this insane thought that Jocelyn came back. What if the young woman changed her mind and was standing by Louise's bed when we entered?

No one was in the room. Louise was awake and was staring at a television show. As we entered the room, I noticed the show was one of Louise's favorites, the *I Love Lucy Show*. Louise laughed out loud and then turned to see us walk into the room. I watched her face light up.

"Eugeena, it's so good to see you. I don't think you've ever come to visit me two days in a row."

I smiled back, my emotions rising up. "It's always good to see you, friend." I looked over at the detective. "Louise, do you remember Detective Wilkes?"

Louise peered at the detective. "Yes, you were the one

investigating Mary's death this past summer. My goodness, what would bring you here?"

I thought I heard Detective Wilkes gulp, but then I
realized that was me. For once I decided to stay quiet and I
looked at the detective.

Detective Wilkes stepped closer to Louise's bed. "Mrs.
Hopkins ..."

Louise interrupted her. "Oh honey, you can call me
Louise."

The detective smiled. "Louise. When was the last time
you saw your son?"

Louise's smile faltered a bit. "Yesterday. Oh no what is
William up to now? That boy told me he found someone
to buy my house. I told him not to go through with it.
All this is happening too fast." Louise started waving her
hands.

Detective Wilkes glanced over at me.

I shuffled closer to Louise's bed and patted her on her
hand. "Louise, you're going to have to listen. Detective
Wilkes has a bit of bad news to share."

Louise held her hand to her chest. "What? Did something happen to William?"

Detective Wilkes cleared her throat. "Your son was
fatally wounded last night at your former home."

*Fatally wounded. That was a real nice way of putting it,
detective.*

Louise frowned. "Is he okay?"

I sighed and shook my head. "No, Louise. William is
gone."

"Gone away."

I closed my eyes. "Gone to be with his father."

"But his father is ..." Louise stopped as she started to
realize what we were trying to tell her. "My boy is dead?"

Both Detective Wilkes and I nodded. There were no words at the moment.

I watched Louise as her eyes grew wide and she clutched her nightgown. "He can't be gone. He was my baby. I tried to be the best mother I could be."

"Oh, Louise, you were a really good mother to William. The best."

Tears flowed down Louise's face. "I'm being punished now."

Punished. I looked back at Detective Wilkes, who was looking at me with questions in her eyes. I shook my head. I didn't know where this was going. "Louise, this isn't punishment. Someone meant William harm."

Louise wailed and held her hands to her face. "It's my fault. I caused this to happen and now I've lost all of my babies."

I looked for Louise's buzzer on the bed. "Louise, maybe I should get you a nurse. I'm so sorry this has happened."

Louise reached out and grabbed my arm with more strength than I knew she had. "Eugeena, I have to make it right."

Detective Wilkes stepped closer. "Make what right? Mrs. Patterson, do you know what she's talking about? Does this have anything to do with what happened to Mr. Hopkins last night?"

Louise seemed to slip right before my eyes as she stared off into space. She whispered something.

I leaned closer to hear what Louise was saying.

"August, I'm so sorry. For everything?"

Who was August? I would have expected Louise to call out her deceased husband's name. For some reason, her distressed mind was on someone named August.

I reached for Louise's hand and tried to loosen her grip

on my arm. "Louise, I don't know what you think you're being punished for, but I'm going to help you get through this."

Louise's shoulders shook as she cried. "It's my fault. My fault."

I reached over and hugged my fragile friend. I looked at Detective Wilkes. "We need a nurse in here."

The detective stared at Louise, nodded that she understood and then left the room.

This was about more than the pain of losing her son; there was something from the past haunting Louise as the same time. I had a feeling I would need to find Jocelyn Miller.

And whoever this August person was to Louise.

Chapter 9

Detective Wilkes and I stood outside Louise's doors. Pat heard the commotion and came in to help settle Louise down. She turned toward us and said, "I gave her something to let her sleep. Poor thing needs to rest. I'm so sorry to hear about her son."

I twisted my hands like a nervous child. "Please keep an eye on her. I will be back to check on her later."

Pat nodded her head. "Sure. You're like family. We will take good care of her. No worries, Mrs. Patterson."

Well, I was worried. Detective Wilkes kept looking at me as though I had committed a crime. I turned to walk away, but that little red-haired gal stayed right by my side.

"What was Mrs. Hopkins talking about before they sedated her?"

I shook my head and kept walking. "How am I supposed to know?"

"You seemed to understand."

I stopped and twirled around. "I was trying to comfort my friend who just lost her beloved son."

"Who's the woman that was here yesterday?"

Okay, that question didn't sound good to me. I stared at the detective and then observed our surroundings. I turned to the front desk to see that Lexi watching us. I bet that no-breaking-the-rules receptionist said something to the detective. I looked on the other side of the desk and saw Ms. Saunders having words with Pat. Pat was looking rather animated. I wondered what had Pat all upset.

Really anyone could have told the detective about Jocelyn. Why did she think it was my duty to tell her? I took a deep breath. "I assume you're referring to the young lady claiming to be Louise's granddaughter?"

Detective Wilkes crossed her arms and looked at me. "You weren't planning to tell me?"

"Detective, no disrespect, but I believe you found out on your own just fine. Now I hope we're finished because I'm upset after seeing my friend in that state." I twirled around and marched towards the front door.

The young detective kept up with my steps, which wasn't hard to do because I wasn't a fast walker. "I'm sorry. I know that was very hard seeing your friend's grief. This is very difficult. Please, I have a few more questions for you. Had you seen the woman before?"

"Never. I didn't know who she was when I saw her."

"Was there animosity between this woman and Mr. Hopkins?"

Now that stopped me in my tracks as my dream from last night floated to the surface. I turned to face the detective. *Really, Eugeena, a man was shot to death last night next door.* A man I had watched grow up alongside my own children. I needed to help this woman the best I could. "Jocelyn was nervous about William showing up. I'm sure she wasn't expecting him because she was trying to meet the woman she thought was her grandmother. William is ...

was an intimidating fellow. He kind of just came in and *we* had to leave."

Detective Wilkes had whipped out her notepad. "Her name is Jocelyn. Last name?"

I felt protective all of a sudden, and I wasn't sure why. I blurted out, "Why do you need to know this? When she left she wanted to forget everything. Her mother didn't even know she was here."

The detective's eyebrow furrowed. "Was William involved with this woman, Jocelyn's mother? Perhaps there was bad blood between the deceased and the mother?"

Oh boy! "Well, Detective, I see you made the same assumption I did. Jocelyn is not William's daughter. Louise hasn't confirmed, but there appears to be another child, a child that Louise gave up many, many years ago."

Detective Wilkes' sleep-deprived eyes grew wide. "That changes everything about this case. There could be all kinds of motives. We need to find this daughter."

"Suppose the woman doesn't want to be found? This other child doesn't have anything to do with William. Remember I told you last night, William was showing off his house to a potential seller. There was a woman that showed up at the house last night."

"Yes, I know and it's my duty to pinpoint who that woman was at the house last night."

Despite my own crazy thoughts, I was now officially worried that Detective Wilkes was barking up the wrong tree. My own daughter was a person of interest in a case a few months ago and I didn't want another young woman to get ambushed because of a desire to connect to kin. "Jocelyn had no reason to come back. She saw her grandmother and that was all she wanted. She sounded like her mother wanted nothing to do with Louise."

"People change their minds. I will be in touch, Mrs. Patterson. Try to stay out of trouble."

I watched the detective walk away from me. I opened my car door and sat down inside for a minute to catch my thoughts. I couldn't argue with Detective Wilkes. Jocelyn could have certainly changed her mind and could have confessed to her mother about her visit yesterday. I still couldn't see what the purpose was for someone pretending to want to buy a house only to kill the seller. Knowing what I knew, William could have gotten himself involved with something shady.

I thought back to yesterday. Jocelyn was in the room and I know she probably heard that William was selling the house to a potential buyer. Still I didn't think that was Jocelyn's voice I heard last night. Or was I just kidding myself. I only met the woman one time.

I drove home feeling haunted by Louise's distraught face. I turned on one of my favorite songs, *Fixit Jesus* by The Canton Spirituals. I wanted to help my friend, but everything that had transpired in the last two days was making my head hurt.

As I parked my car in my driveway, I heard my phone ringing from my pocketbook. I don't know how long it had been ringing since I did have the music kind of loud. The voicemail had already picked up. While I waited to retrieve the voicemail message I looked up to see Amos outside raking the leaves in front of my yard.

That man had become my yard man, handyman, dinner companion, and in some ways, one of my dearest friends. I'd never imagined at my age that I would have a man as a friend.

Just a friend!

I sat in the car and watched Amos raking leaves until he looked up and waved. I waved back and held my head down. No need to have the man catching me in the act of checking him out. I looked down at my phone and saw the voicemail indicator. I didn't recognize the phone number. I clicked the button and listened to the message.

"Ms. Eugeena, this is Pat, when you get a chance, I really need to talk to you. I think you're the only one who can help."

Help? What is going on that Pat would call me? I wondered if I should turn around and go back to the nursing home.

Someone tapped on my driver side window, startling me. I looked up to see Amos peering down at me with the rake in his hand. I don't know what it was with him and overalls. That seemed to be his uniform. He opened the car door and held it open for me.

"How did things go with Louise?"

I placed the phone in my bag and pulled myself out of the car. Amos closed the car door and we walked back toward my porch. "Not too well. I knew she would be upset about William, but I have to say something else was upsetting her too." I stopped and looked at Amos. "I think Jocelyn stirred up something in Louise. She mentioned how she lost all her babies. You know she had a miscarriage in her first marriage, but I can't help but feel like she was referring to another child. A third child."

Amos leaned the rake against the side of the house and lifted his baseball cap off his bald head. "You're not thinking of trying to find this Jocelyn. Didn't she want to leave it all alone?"

"I have to find Jocelyn and her mother." I added in a lower voice. "At least before Detective Wilkes does."

Amos eyed me. "Why? What did you say to the detective?"

I shook my head. "Nothing. Detective Wilkes was already there talking to the staff. She knew a young woman claiming to be Louise's granddaughter came to visit yesterday. Except the detective thought what I thought, that maybe this was William's child. I had to correct her."

"So now this young lady or her mother is a possible suspect?"

"Detective Wilkes seemed interested and thought it put a different angle on the case." I walked up the steps to my porch and then stopped when I reached the top. "You know something else and I don't think I mentioned this to the detective, but William did seem to recognize Jocelyn."

Amos placed his hat back on his head and grabbed the rake. "You know the police should handle this. You don't know what you're really getting into here."

"But I need to warn Jocelyn."

"You don't really know if there is a true DNA relation here. You're going by a resemblance in a photograph. Louise has not confirmed anything."

"I could make sure Jocelyn's story really checked out. Last thing I would want is to cause more grief for Louise."

Amos pointed his finger at me. "Eugeena, you need to think carefully before you jump into this situation. If this was an adoption, there were reasons that happened over fifty years ago. There is no guarantee this will be a happy family reunion. It sounds like Jocelyn recognized that yesterday after meeting William. Don't get any deeper into this until you get more confirmation from Louise especially with William's death center stage now."

Amos made perfectly good sense, but my nosiness had

taken over. This was one of those secrets to which I wanted the whole story.

Chapter 10

Tuesdays were blog days for me. With my sixtieth birthday coming up, I was quite tickled to be able to refer to myself as a blogger. I had inherited my son Cedric's old laptop and with some help from his girlfriend, Carmen, I've been able to publish at least one blog post a week. At first I wasn't sure what to write. When I learned I had diabetes, I discovered the best way to learn how to manage my disease was to talk with others online. There was so much information I decided to share my finds on a blog at Eugeena-Patterson.com. I wasn't world famous, but I liked having something purposeful to do.

Today, I published a post that I needed for me, but hoped it would help someone. I decided to title the blog post, "Ms. Eugeena's Guide to Breathing or Waiting to Exhale?"

I can credit Amos for my first bullet point.

Think before you jump into someone else's mess.

Of course, my problem at this point was I had overthought whether or not to start trouble. I kind of figured when I walked into Louise's room on Sunday and found

Jocelyn leaning over the bed that trouble had found me. A murder right next door escalated the trouble factor to another degree. I was never one of those people who had an easy time letting things go. But I knew I needed to stop and breathe.

Writing calmed my nerves to a degree. I re-read my blog post again, and then I hit publish to share it with the World Wide Web. I took a peek at my Facebook and Twitter account to see if the new blog post was posted. I was really proud of myself because a few months ago, I barely checked email. Who had time to do that stuff in between grading papers?

Now I had apps on my phone and I was just Ms. Tech Savvy. I stopped patting myself on my back long enough to remember I was savvy with Google too.

I typed in Jocelyn Miller in Google to see what came up. There were a lot of women with the same name. Some trashy looking women too. Since that search didn't work, I went over to Facebook. I had found quite a few classmates by typing in their name. Some of them I really didn't want to contact, but I was curious about what they had been up to all these years. It was amazing what people posted out there in public. *My goodness!*

After I typed in Jocelyn's name, I saw a few photos come up. Just as I found a photo that looked like the young woman I met Sunday, the phone rang. I ignored the phone for a minute and pulled up Jocelyn's Facebook page. She was a really pretty girl. The phone kept ringing as I thought whether or not it would be a good idea to do a friend request. If I did, wouldn't that make me appear like I was stalking her? Of course, that's kind of what I was doing.

I held that thought and went to grab the phone. When

I saw who was on the caller ID I was actually grateful for the interruption. I picked up the phone, "Well, Cora, you called just in time because I have myself in a bit of predicament."

The closest person to being a sister to me was also my aunt. Cora Gibson was only two years older than me and the youngest child in the Gibson clan. She answered me back, "You and Amos finally went out on that date yet?"

"No," I sputtered. "What is it with everyone and this matchmaking? Leave me and Amos alone. Please don't tell me you called me to ask me that."

Cora laughed. "Girl, I thought you were getting with it."

"Getting with what? Cora, you and I are not spring chickens. I've lived my life."

"But you still have more years to live and there's nothing wrong with being happy. Now what have you gotten yourself into now?"

I took the cordless phone and sank down in the living room chair to catch Cora up on what all had happened.

"Oh my! Who knew your little ole neighbor had that much drama in her life? Do you know who the father could be?"

I shook my head. "I have no idea, but Louise mentioned the name August yesterday. She didn't give a last name, nor did she confirm, but I assumed this was someone special. Could be the father of this baby girl."

I was really just talking out loud. I did that quite often when I talked to Cora. She knew me and would add her two cents when necessary. "The more I think about it Louise had to be in her teens when she had this baby girl. She married her first husband at age eighteen. When that marriage didn't work out, she married her second husband at age twenty-three and had William maybe a year later."

Louise's story of having a child in her teens wasn't too different from mine. My oldest son's conception prompted the shotgun wedding between Ralph and me. I had to finish school and later went back after having Cedric. I was still a bit upset that Louise never thought to mention this to me in all the years we had known each other. But there had to be significant reasons.

"Cora, you know something else? During Louise's time, I imagine they hid girls away for a while until a baby was born and given away for adoption."

Cora spoke up. "They certainly did. Did Louise grow up around here, Eugeena?"

"Yes, Louise has been in Charleston all her life. In fact, I do know her ancestors owned a plantation in Charleston, so she has no problem tracking her roots. Remember I told you she always tried to downplay that part of her life."

"That's right. Well, you know Esther might be able to shine some light on this fellow named August. Esther knows everyone around here and people know her."

Aunt Esther was the oldest of my father's siblings and my godmother. How the oldest and the youngest child were still left out of eight children was amazing since the two women were quite alike in many ways. In her eighties, Esther was still quite feisty and didn't mind giving her baby sister, Cora, a hard time. In recent months, Cora had taken on becoming Esther's caregiver. Being a former nurse, it seemed like a good fit, but those two ladies could get on each other's nerves pretty good, often times with Cora calling me to keep her sanity.

"You know I do need to pay you ladies a visit. It's been awhile. I want to ask Louise what happened all those years ago, but William's death has put her in a bit of tailspin too. I mean someone shot the man next door to me."

"Girl, your neighborhood has gone down a bit. What have the kids said?"

I smacked my forehead with my hand. "I haven't told any of them. I guess I better before I have one or all of them showing up to my door, especially Junior. I think he went to school about two years behind William."

"Oh girl, you know that oldest boy will try to move you out of that house if he could. How is everyone else doing anyway? I can't believe Thanksgiving will be here in six weeks."

"You are telling me. Even though I'm out of the classroom, time is still flying by. You know Junior's wife should be having their third baby boy around Christmas. Leesa has been doing pretty good. She came by for Sunday dinner with Kisha and Tyric. Both of those munchkins are grow-ing fast." I sighed. "The only child of mine that I haven't heard from or seen has been Cedric. Since him and you know who moved in together, he's become a stranger."

"Now Eugeena, you're not still fussing about that boy being unmarried, although he is almost forty, right?"

"Cora, that is what doesn't make any sense to me. All this time Cedric has never shacked up with a woman. Sud-denly this girl is special. Okay, well that is wonderful, but when did marriage become so unpopular?" I held my hand to my head as if to ward off a headache. "Don't get me started if he gets that Carmen girl pregnant. I already feel sometimes I flat out failed as a parent with Leesa. I believe I was just tired when that girl came along."

"Now let's not go there, Eugeena. There's no need to be hard on yourself. You and Ralph did the best you could do. Besides, you never know, sometimes playing house might encourage them to do the real thing. That girl is a bit younger than Cedric. I imagine she would want a ring after a while."

Cora had a point. There was at least a ten-year difference in Cedric and Carmen's age, which I always found pretty fascinating as well.

I turned from my thoughts to hear Cora's laughter.

"What's so funny," I asked.

"You have more going on now than when you were in the classroom teaching. You sound like you're enjoying retirement just fine."

I walked back over to the computer and sat down. "The superintendent did ask me if I wanted to substitute teach sometime, but I honestly have plenty to keep me busy."

Maybe a bit too much.

I peered at Jocelyn's Facebook page and noticed she had just posted a status. I leaned in to read what she posted and sucked in a breath.

Have you ever done something unforgivable?

I gulped as I scanned the comments below her post. Like a few of those who posted comments, I wanted to know what Jocelyn had done.

Cora's voice invaded my paranoid thoughts, "Eugeena, are you okay? What's going on with you? Have you monitored your sugar today?"

"What? Yes, my glucose levels were normal. I will be eating in a bit. Look I have to go. I will keep you updated on what's going on around here."

"Alright, Eugeena. Just play it safe. You almost got yourself killed the last time you were digging around."

"Believe me this is nothing like the last time. I hope to see you and Aunt Esther soon. Goodbye, Cora." I hung up the phone thinking to myself at least I hoped to see them soon.

If Detective Wilkes caught sight of the status Jocelyn just posted, that girl would surely be moved to the top of the suspect list. Why'd did people post such things publicly? Was this a cry for help?

I didn't know whether she would respond, but I decided to send Jocelyn a message on Facebook. *Jocelyn, this is Eugeena Patterson. I met you on Sunday at Hillcrest Manor Nursing Home. It's urgent you get in touch with me as soon as possible.*

Chapter 11

About an hour went by and I was still looking at the Facebook. I can't believe how you can waste hours just clicking and looking at other people's Facebook pages. I was really wondering what Jocelyn had done that she thought was unforgivable. I just couldn't wrap my head around murder. There was no doubt a woman was the shooter, but that wasn't Jocelyn's car over at the house. That was clue number two for me whether it made sense or not.

The more I thought about it, it felt like poor William was set up. Did the woman really want to buy Louise's house or was she looking for a way to trap poor William for another reason? William wasn't the most respectable guy. I suspected, even though I had never shared with Louise, that her boy was really a con artist. He could talk his way out of just about anything especially with his mother who seemed to dote on him just a bit too much. Now Mr. Hopkins wasn't easily fooled, and I remembered Louise was worried that her husband was not very proud of William.

Bill Hopkins had good reason to suspect his son of not having much integrity.

I checked the time on my laptop and saw it was way after lunch. I went to the kitchen and fixed a peanut butter sandwich. As I gulped down the sandwich, I decided I better contact my oldest son first about William's shooting. While Junior had his own family, he had taken the role of stepping into his father's shoes seriously. A few months ago, I had a serious conversation with him about the safety of the neighborhood. If he found out about William's death by some other way, he would certainly drive from Greenville to Charleston and give me that same lecture again.

As a successful, busy corporate lawyer, I usually wasn't sure if Junior was in court or the office, so I tried calling his office first. As the phone ring, I kept wondering if Jocelyn would message me back on Facebook. She probably was thinking she needed to stay far away from *that cuckoo Eugeena Patterson.*

I mean I could technically be considered a stalker since I tracked her down.

My son's secretary picked up the phone saving me from drifting into even more foolish thinking. "Ralph Patterson's office."

"Yes Aimee, this is his mother, Mrs. Eugeena Patterson. Is Mr. Patterson available?"

"Hello, Mrs. Patterson, it's so good to hear from you. Let me check to see if Mr. Patterson is available."

A few moments later, a deep voice boomed over the phone. "Mama, is everything all right?"

"Everything is okay here, but I thought I better call you before you found out."

"Found out? Mama, that's not good to hear. Now you have me alarmed."

I gulped. I've had the opportunity to see my son arguing a case. He was quite the formidable opponent being a large man with a tendency for the dramatic. I braced myself because I knew Junior was going to turn that dramatic flair up a notch when he heard my news. "Now, Junior, I don't need you to run up your blood pressure."

I could picture Junior's large frame taking a breath as he sighed. "That advice is not helping me, Mama, but I'm listening."

"There was a tragic incident last night. William Hopkins is dead."

"How? I just saw him a few weeks ago."

I started to tell Junior the details of William's shooting, but stopped. "What? Where did you see him?"

"That doesn't matter now if the man's dead, Mama."

"Excuse me, but any clues to why the man was shot to death would be important."

"Shot? William was murdered? Where?"

I was starting to see telling Junior might not have been a good idea because I felt my own blood pressure rising. I took a deep breath, and decided to wait before I told Junior that William was shot to death next door.

Baby steps, Eugeena.

"Junior, why don't you tell me about the last time you saw William. Was there anything different about him?"

"Why do I feel like you're not telling me everything, Mama?"

It was time to pull mama rank. "Ralph, Jr., tell me about William. His mama has lost her only child, and any clues would help the police."

Junior was quiet for a moment. "Alright, I don't need

you getting upset either. I saw William about two weeks ago when I was visiting a client in Charleston."

I frowned. "You were in Charleston and didn't come see me?"

"Mama, it was a quick day trip. Anyhow, William was coming out of the building that I was entering. I almost didn't recognize him. The only clue was I thought I recognized William's voice. He has that way of talking through his nose that's pretty distinct. He was saying to the guy, 'This is going to be a successful venture.' I turned around and I hate to say it but I was probably staring. William ... well he looked different. Being curious, I waited for him to finish talking to the man."

"Man? Had you seen him before?"

"In fact, yes, I've seen the guy William was speaking to in a couple of publications. He's a young guy who grew up around in South Carolina, went off to some Ivy League school and decided to set up business down here. His name is Jake something. Can't think of his last name at the moment. Walks around with a hoodie so you wouldn't know he was a businessman."

"Is that so? Could you tell what else they were talking about?"

"Why so many questions, Mama?"

"Junior?"

"No, Mama, you need to tell me everything or I'm going to have to visit or better yet call Mr. Amos. I know he will give me the 4-1-1."

"Why in the world would you call Amos?"

"Mr. Amos keeps an eye on you for us."

What? I didn't know whether or not to be offended. It was one thing that Cora, Leesa and Louise were trying to play matchmaker, but my sons had made Amos a spy. *The nerve of these people.*

Junior continued, not knowing the turmoil he just caused. "Anyway, if your inquiring mind must know, I think ole Will was surprised to see me, but he seemed pretty excited to spill the news about his investment in some technology startup company. I guess this Jake fellow is one of the partners. I reminded William that I deal with corporate law and if he had any questions feel free to look me up."

"An investment in a startup? Here in Charleston?"

"Yep, right in your backyard. Charleston has really grown in the past decade and has been called the Silicon Harbor."

"Wow, well I didn't know that." Still I was thinking there had to be a lot of money at stake. Where was William getting that kind of money to invest in a company? I knew he had power of attorney over Louise's estate and money. Louise came from money, but it didn't strike me that she was *that* wealthy for her son to mess over her money.

I shook my head. "This sounds like risky business to me. You said William appeared to look different?"

"He looked really clean, dressed in a real expensive suit. I didn't think it was William's style."

"That's what I thought when I saw him on Sunday."

"You saw William before his death? What exactly are you up to, Mama? You're not snooping around are you?"

"I'm head of the neighborhood watch, Junior. I keep up with incidents like this."

"What would William's death have to do with the neighborhood watch?"

I sighed deeply. "I haven't told you everything. William was trying to sell Louise's house. There was a buyer next door the night William was killed. You see there was a woman –"

"Mama, are you saying William was killed next door to you?"

I couldn't see him, but I'm pretty sure Junior just lifted himself off his seat. I said quietly, "I wasn't in danger. Amos was here."

"I'm glad Mr. Amos was there to help protect you, but we don't need you getting yourself into trouble again, Mama."

I rolled my eyes. I hadn't told Junior everything, but at this point, I needed to re-read that little blog post I wrote earlier about stress. "You touch base with Amos, if you want. Everything is fine, so there's no need for you to be blowing your top at work."

Junior sighed deeply as if disappointed in me. "I just want you to be careful, Mama."

"Don't worry about me. Look, if you get a chance to find out the name of that company or anything else about this Jake fellow, let me know. I need to check on Louise now."

"Alright, Mama. I will see what I can do. Goodbye."

I hung up the phone thinking I need to warn Amos that Junior was going to call. Quite frankly I didn't realize either of my sons had Amos' phone number.

I picked the phone back up and dialed the nursing home. A voice answered that sounded familiar to me. "Hillcrest Manor Nursing Home, this is Jacqueline Saunders speaking, how may I help you?"

"Yes, Mrs. Saunders I ran into you yesterday. I wanted to check on Louise Hopkins to see how she was doing today."

It sounded like the nursing home director was talking to someone else.

"Mrs. Saunders, are you still there?"

"Yes, Mrs. Patterson, it was good to meet you yesterday. I'm sorry but Mrs. Hopkins won't be able to take visitors for a while. She's really been distraught and we're watching her carefully."

I frowned. "Oh my! I hate to hear that. Well, when can I come to see her?"

"Why don't you check back in a few days? Maybe you would like to view our facilities. We have so many new improvements for our residents. Oh! There's another call. Thank you for calling Hillcrest Manor Nursing Home."

I heard a click in my ear. I stared at the phone. *Was that woman trying to sell me something?* I put the phone down.

I know I left Louise in a pretty bad state yesterday, but I was feeling a bit alarmed that I couldn't see her. My first instinct was to call back or better yet drive over to the nursing home. But then I remembered Louise's distraught face and her calling out for August yesterday. It was probably best not to upset her any further.

I might not be able to see Louise at the moment, but I could certainly do what I could to find answers about her son's death. Since I wasn't one to sit around and twiddle my thumbs, I knew just the person to go visit instead.

Chapter 12

My first thought after I parked at the Charleston Police Department was that I might should have consulted with Amos about what I was about to do. As I climbed out of the car, I told myself I knew exactly what I was doing because Amos would have calmly talked me out of going to talk to Detective Wilkes. He would have warned me how she wouldn't share any information and how I should let *her* handle the case.

I had no issues with any of those suggestions. I was left with the feeling that Detective Wilkes had some other ideas that could waste valuable time. She didn't have a good understanding of the victim. I believed William, unknowingly, invited his killer to take advantage of him. I just couldn't come up with the motive. William had been floating around Lord knows where like an overgrown Peter Pan for well over a decade. Why suddenly decide it was time to grow up? What was the investment and who was this partner?

I also had other questions. Was William planning to stay here in Charleston after all these years? Once again I questioned why he put Louise in the nursing home, and why sell a house that's been in his family for years?

I entered the police station and went to the front desk. A short officer leaned across the counter. He was graying around the temples and his hairline was receding. He wore his hair in a buzz cut which made his puffy cheeks look not quite as tough as he might have wanted it to appear. He stared at me. "Can I help you, ma'am?"

"Yes, I'm looking for Detective Wilkes. I have some information about the William Hopkins case."

The officer whose badge read, Officer Gonzalez, responded, "I will see if she's in. Have a seat over there?" He pointed to hardback plastic chairs across from the desk.

I decided to stand and smiled. "I'll wait here, son."

The officer raised his eyebrow, but picked up the phone. "Your name, ma'am?"

"Eugeena Patterson."

I looked around as he called Detective Wilkes.

Officer Gonzalez placed the phone down and said, "She will be here in a few minutes."

"Thank you."

A few minutes later, Detective Wilkes walked up to me looking weary, with deep circles under her eyes. How could she solve a crime appearing this sleep-deprived?

I frowned, "Honey, do you ever sleep?"

Detective Wilkes barely smiled and her left eye seemed to have a tick going. "I have been suffering a bit of insomnia as of late. What do you have for me, Mrs. Patterson?"

"Well, when you left yesterday, you didn't really ask information specifically about William. You are going to look into his activities prior to his... well, murder?"

"Mrs. Patterson, I promise you I will turn over every aspect of the victim's life."

"What about his sudden access to money?"

Detective Wilkes frowned. "Did Mrs. Hopkins say anything to you?"

"No, but I've known William since he was this high." I brought my hand to my hip. "He's always had his hand out for money and has lived a rather nomadic lifestyle that's led him to all *kinds* of people. Louise is not lacking in finances and it's my understanding William had power of attorney over his mother's money."

"Okay, I do understand Mr. Hopkins traveled a bit and he seems to have enjoyed access to money."

"I'm glad you picked up on that too? Do you remember when Louise got hurt this past summer and her son showed up at the hospital?"

Detective Wilkes shook her head. "I don't know if I remember seeing her son then."

"Oh you did, you probably just didn't match that unkempt man with the ragged ponytail with the one you found on Sunday evening in a very expensive suit."

Detective Wilkes seemed to perk up for a slight minute. Her eyes flashed. "Okay I get it. Mr. Hopkins definitely had a change in his lifestyle. Mrs. Patterson, I appreciate –"

I held up my hands as though I could physically stop her from dismissing me, "There's more you should know. According to my sources, William had a business partner and they were investing in something big, some technology startup company here in Charleston." I didn't need to let Detective Wilkes know my source was my son.

The detective frowned. "Your source? That's interesting, Mrs. Patterson."

"You do know you can call me Eugeena, right?"

The detective shook her head as if she was trying to shake something out of her ears. "Mrs... Eugeena. Look, I'm really glad you came by to enlighten me about William's lifestyle. I will certainly look into all of this."

I eyed her and asked, "But you're still thinking Jocelyn Miller's showing up on Sunday is highly suspicious."

"Eugeena." The detective folded her arms. "I can't share anything about this case with you."

I started to twist my hands. "I just don't want any more heartache to come to this family. There's a chance that Louise may want to connect with this family and I hate for there to be anything hanging over their heads about William's death."

"That's not my intentions." Detective Wilkes' green eyes flashed as she looked off in another direction and then back at me. "You know now that you're here, I have a question for you."

"Oh."

"On Sunday, you mentioned that Mr. Hopkins and Ms. Miller met each other."

"There weren't any official introductions, but they saw each other."

Detective Wilkes leaned in. "I need you to answer this honestly. Did you get any sense that Mr. Hopkins knew Ms. Miller?"

I sucked in a breath. Sometimes I couldn't stop my reactions if I tried. I had sense enough not to blurt out what first came to mind.

Detective Wilkes looked at me intensely. "Eugeena?"

I let out a sigh. "I don't want you to take anything out of context."

"I'm here to pull facts and clues together so I can solve

a murder. The tiniest of details can determine if a killer is caught."

I swallowed. "William was interested in Jocelyn, I thought because he wanted to know who she was. I mean if some strange woman was visiting my mother's bedside, I would ask the same thing."

"What did Mr. Hopkins ask?"

"He asked who she was and then a few minutes later he asked if he'd seen her some place before?"

Detective Wilkes seemed to come alive like the Energizer Bunny. "He recognized her?"

"He seemed *to think* he recognized her, but I told you Jocelyn was not the woman at the house on Sunday night."

"But neither you nor Mr. Jones saw anyone in the dark."

I desperately wanted to make sure the detective wasn't going to continue spinning down this path. "I did hear a woman's voice and I'm pretty sure I would have recognized Jocelyn's voice."

Detective Wilkes shook her head. "I've dealt with a lot of witnesses and you would be surprised what you remember or don't remember." The detective extended her arm to shake my hand. "Eugeena, once again I appreciate you stopping by. Having citizens assist with finding clues really helps solve crimes."

I looked down at the detective's hand and shook it. I wasn't finished yet although I doubt she would tell me. "Do you have something that proves William and Jocelyn met each other before Sunday?"

The detective looked at me solemnly. "Eugeena, I don't need to tell you that people aren't always how they appear."

With that the petite detective walked off leaving me wondering what in the world had the detective found out.

Chapter 13

After returning home, I was even more anxious that Jocelyn hadn't returned my message on Facebook. I imagined she chose to ignore my message. I'm not sure if that was a good thing or not after what Detective Wilkes told me. Or rather didn't tell me. Why did William think he recognized Jocelyn? What did Jocelyn do that she would post such a foolish status on Facebook?

Based on my conversation earlier with Junior, I tried to search for companies in Charleston to get an idea of what technology companies were here. I had no idea that Charleston had become more than a tourist town with its deep history and ghost tours.

I eventually grew tired of surfing. As I slept, another fit of dreams involving Louise, William and Jocelyn haunted me. In the dream, Louise was standing on her porch like she used to with her hands clutched over her chest. She kept looking back and forth down the street. William was approaching from one side and Jocelyn from the other side of the street. They were walking down the street like they were in gun fight to see which one of them would draw their weapon first. When Jocelyn reached for her gun, that's when the phone woke me up.

I peered at the big numbers on my clock displaying it was seven o'clock in the morning. It wasn't quite day-light yet, but I could tell the sun was trying to do some-thing. I reached for the phone which by now I suspected was on the fourth ring, right before it goes to voicemail. I hated when that happened because sometimes I forgot to check the voicemail. Usually when I did remember to check voicemail it was one of my children leaving a frantic message about me not picking up the phone.

I picked up the phone. "Hello."

"Eugeena, oh, did I wake you?"

I shook my head and then remembered Cora couldn't see me. "I'm not quite awake yet, but what's going on. Is everything okay?"

"Yes and no. I was talking to Esther last night about your friend. She got really animated when I mentioned the name August. You should come today. She wouldn't tell me anything else. She just said, 'Eugeena needs to know the whole story.'"

What story? That changed my plans for the day. It was Wednesday. I felt like I should try to see how Louise was doing. I didn't want her to feel abandoned and I was really concerned about her mental state. When Cora said Esther wanted me to come, like a child I dropped everything to see what my auntie and godmother wanted. I hastily got up and dressed.

Poor Porgy was running around until I finally stopped and let him do his thing out in the backyard. Once Porgy was settled, I grabbed some oatmeal because I didn't dare leave the house without some food in me. I would need the energy. It sounded like it was a good day for Aunt Esther's mind. She would be sharp and focused. We had quite a few school teachers in the family. Esther was the first person in our family to become a teacher. She instilled in me the desire and love for education and history.

It was still pretty early and the wind was up today. The fall weather was trying to settle in the South. As I inched my way down the steps, I looked next door. I had a distant memory of Louise bundled up in her down coat feeding a stray cat. She was a gentle soul, though quite the nosy neighbor, she meant well. I felt helpless being so close to a crime with no clues.

I climbed in my car and glanced over at Amos' house. I wondered if he was up yet. It was well past eight o'clock. His house was quiet, but I'm sure he was bustling around in there. So many people had left the neighborhood and others may continue to go. I certainly didn't want to leave my home. When the murder happened a few months ago, my oldest boy wanted to move me out of the home where I raised all three of my children. I just couldn't do that.

Plus, I was nowhere near helpless. I turned on my car ignition and headed towards my aunt's house, which was only twenty minutes away. As I drove, my thoughts wandered to what Esther would share with me. It was quite strange that this August person had been on Louise's mind. My friend must have been thinking quite a bit about the past after Jocelyn's visit on Sunday.

Then it occurred to me. Suppose this August person was still alive? Had Jocelyn tried to reach or find any information about who could be her maternal grandfather too?

As I drew closer to my aunt's house, my own past memories were stirred. When most of the family was still living, my aunt's house was where we gathered for the holidays and family reunions. I parked my car in front of the Gibson family house that was painted in of all colors, Pepto-Bismol® pink. Growing up, the house was a pale yellow. I don't remember whose idea it was to paint the house pink.

I knocked on the door and waited. Cora opened it. "Girl, it's good to see you." She stepped back and looked at me. "You look like you haven't been sleeping."

I waved her off and stepped inside. "I'm fine. Is Aunt Esther up?"

A strong, melodic voice floated from the living room. "Is that you, Eugeena?"

"Yes, ma'am." I went into the living room to where Esther sat in a chair. Most of the people in my family were pretty tall. My sons received their height from their dad and my side of the family. Most of the women were more average in height like me. Esther was the tallest of all the women. Never married, she was a regal woman who carried herself with pride. She reminded me a lot of Maya Angelou.

Esther's silver hair was cropped short and reminded me of a halo. She had a blanket wrapped around her. I noticed Esther was holding her worn bible. I believe Esther had that leather King James bible since I was a young woman and that's been a long time. The pages were barely intact and sticking out in various places.

I crossed the room to hug her. "How are you doing, Auntie?"

"As good as I can be. You taking care of yourself, girlie?" Esther frowned at me, but there was a hint of amusement tugging at her lips. "What's this I hear about you having a boyfriend?"

I swung around and glared at Cora. Cora sat down on the couch with a huge grin on her face. I turned back toward my aunt making note of the sly smile on Esther's face. The sight of that smile was pretty rare, but I was still a bit embarrassed.

"Well, I see you two have been talking about me. What has Cora Gibson been telling you?" I sat down on the couch on the other end of the couch so I could be closer to Aunt Esther. "I don't know why your younger sister feels like she must create a soap opera out of other people's lives."

Cora leaned in. "Esther, she cooks for him. I would say he's something special."

I huffed. "The man has to eat. Besides he helps me keep up with my yard and broken things around the house. I am on a fixed income now."

Cora arched her eyebrow. "I'm sure it's nice to have a man around the house."

I waved Cora away like she was a gnat. "Just ignore her. Aunt Esther, since Cora is keeping you in the know about my business, I assume she told you about my neighbor?"

Aunt Esther nodded. "She did. It brought to my mind an incident I had almost forgotten about."

I frowned. "What incident? Sounds serious."

Aunt Esther was quiet for a moment. She laid her bible on the table in front of her and patted it as though she was drawing some type of strength. I looked over at Cora, who glanced at me and then back to her older sister. We both waited.

Aunt Esther started to rock her chair as she pulled the blanket closer to her chest. "You remember the time you had the family reunion at your house, Eugeena?"

"Yes, that was about fifteen years ago, Aunt Esther."

"That wasn't the first time I met your neighbor, Louise."

"Really?" It was the first and last time I hosted a family reunion at the house. I tried to erase memories of that event. Ralph and I were at each other's throats, but we put on the best fish fry ever. Many people in the neighborhood showed up at our reunion, pretending to be kinfolks. With her blue eyes and blond hair, Louise kind of stood out, but she made herself right at home. "I remember you seemed to think you'd seen Louise before. She kept saying no this was the first time you two had met."

"I rarely forget faces." Aunt Esther pointed to Cora. "When Cora mentioned something about an August fellow, then I started to remember. You see I've only known one man, well really a boy back then, named August in my life. He was a student of mine and *that* August didn't have a good ending."

"Ending?" I sat up straight and asked, "What do you mean?"

"August Manning. August was a great baseball player, touted to be the next great Jackie Robinson around here. He wasn't too bad with his school work. He could have gone a long way except..."

I leaned forward. "Don't keep us in suspense, Aunt Esther."

Esther's held her hand to her chest as if the thought made her uncomfortable. "August's life was cut short. In a very violent way."

"He was murdered?" I frowned. Now I was certainly not expecting to hear that and hoped for once that Aunt Esther was wrong.

Chapter 14

Esther folded her hands in her lap and continued, "There was a rumor that August had become involved with a young white girl. You know, back then it wasn't good for a black man to be around a white woman. I recalled seeing a young blond-haired woman around August one evening after a game. I asked him about his *friend*, and even tried to gently warn him that he and the young woman should be getting along separately to their own homes."

Esther stopped talking, she picked at the blanket around her. She finally continued, looking straight ahead. "A few days later, someone or maybe more than one person, had gotten hold of August. Whoever it was beat August senseless and left him for dead near the same base-ball field where he broke records and hit home runs."

As the reality of what Esther told us sank in, I blinked thinking this was worse than I thought. I asked, "Why would you think this was the same August? Louise didn't give me a last name. I know you don't forget faces, but suppose the girl you remembered wasn't the same Louise. That was so long ago."

Esther looked at me. "It was her eyes. That girl with August had the bluest eyes I had ever seen. Something about Louise's eyes made me think I'd seen her before." Esther leaned forward and asked, "This girl that came to see Louise on Sunday, did she appear to be mixed or what we called back in the day, mulatto?"

I nodded. "Yes, but her mother was married to an African American man." I reached into my purse. "Here is the photo of Jocelyn's mother."

Esther took the photo. Cora scrambled off the couch to stand behind her sister to view the photo. Both Esther and Cora studied the photo for a long time. Finally, Esther handed the photo back to me.

"There is only one way to really know. You should ask your friend, but I can tell you I see August Manning in that woman's face too. She could be his daughter. Cora, go in my room and bring me that black leather album that sits on the top of my dresser."

Cora sped off like she was much younger than her sixty-two years. I twisted my hands and waited in silence to see what else Esther had for me.

Cora returned with a large black leather album. There were papers and photos sticking out. Esther took the album. She must have already pulled out what she wanted me to see, because she flipped it open and handed me a photo.

I looked at her and then Cora before reaching over to take the photo.

The photo was a black and white of a very handsome dark-skinned young man. He wore a baseball hat and appeared to be dressed in uniform. His smile was bright and teeth perfectly straight in the photo. I sensed the warmth and kindness in his eyes and *that* smile.

For a brief moment, I felt a deep sense of sadness pass over me even though I didn't know the man or had ever seen him before. I cleared my throat. "This is August."

Esther nodded.

I held the photo next to Jocelyn's family photo. I wasn't sure how to feel at that moment knowing how August had died. Suddenly, I started to understand why Jocelyn felt a need not to dig into the past. If she'd found out any of the information I had just found, or even if her mother knew, that had to be pretty devastating.

A thought popped into my mind. I wiped my eyes not realizing I had really been affected with a growing sense of anger. "This happened in 1964. So August's murder has been unsolved for fifty years? No one had any idea who was involved."

Esther looked down in her lap. She lifted her head. "There were at least two boys that people in the community suspected. Chuck Nelson and ..."

I leaned forward. "And?"

Esther stared at me. "I believe the other one was Bill Hopkins."

"Bill? Louise's husband? Well, that would be crazy. Bill was a great guy and neighbor. She certainly wouldn't have married him if she knew he had anything to do with something that horrendous."

Lord, how could someone live with themselves?

Cora shook her head. "Maybe she didn't know. It sounds like it was just a rumor. Right, Esther?"

"Those are the names I remember. They hung out together and played baseball too. Now that I think about it the one that August had a run-in with before his death was the Nelson fellow. He was average height, but a real muscular fellow. He and August were in competition for the most home runs."

Chuck Nelson. For some reason that name was familiar to me, but it wasn't coming to me. Why? I let out a deep sigh. I was tired and it wasn't even noon yet. I wasn't sure it was a good idea to get something heavy like this laid on your psyche in the morning. "Esther, did anyone question these boys?"

Esther shook her head. "Not that I know of. Those rumors were mainly in *our* community. August's sisters still live in the same house. If they're up to it, maybe they can talk to you more about their brother. They used to hold a memorial for him every year, but they haven't done that in years now that they are both up in age."

I might need to pay August's sisters a visit. The pain of someone else's life being taken away so ruthlessly and with no closure. That kind of guilt weighed heavily on a person's soul. I wondered if Louise knew the boys responsible. Did she know her own husband could have been involved?

Who knew that Sugar Creek's resident busybody had so much going on in her own life? Now I was starting to see why Louise never breathed a word of her past life to me all these years. *Oh poor Louise.*

Chapter 15

The rest of my visit with Cora and Esther was pretty somber. Cora knew not to do any more teasing. I think she was just as surprised as I was about the story Aunt Esther revealed. As I drove home I tried to process all that I had learned in the past three days.

There was no way I could talk to Louise and dredge up that kind of pain. It was bad enough as long as William's murder remained a mystery, a funeral would be delayed. I still couldn't wrap my head around Bill. He was a gentle soul although I must say he wasn't as friendly with us as his new neighbors, at first. But then neither was Louise. People can change. We all eventually grew on each other. Bill and Ralph developed a friendship and went to the golf course together.

I really wanted to talk to Amos, but he kind of warned me to not go digging. It wasn't like I really had been digging though. Aunt Esther provided me with another whole layer to Louise's life that I would have never saw coming. How did it all, if any, connect?

It was late in the afternoon when I arrived home. The

days were getting shorter and I felt the need to bump up the temperature in the house when I opened the front door. I slumped into the living room chair. I felt something warm and furry circling around my legs and looked down to see Porgy making himself comfortable next to my feet. I bent over and patted him on the head.

"How are you doing, fellow? I think me and you need a pretty quiet evening."

The house phone rang next to me.

Not only did the house phone ring, but my cell phone was ringing from my bag.

That figures as soon as I proclaim the need for a quiet evening, all the phones would ring. My first thought was to ignore both phones, but I decided to go for the house phone first. What if it was one of my children or my grand-children? Sometimes when it was inconvenient, you have to do what's right in your spirit, not your feelings. Plus, I really can't stand those persistent phone calls that came when you were too tired to care who was on the other end. That just pushed me into a grumpier state.

I struggled up from the chair and reached over for the phone on what I knew was the last ring before voicemail. "Hello."

"Ms. Eugeena, are you okay? It's Carmen."

That caught my attention. To have my son's girlfriend and housemate calling me out of the blue was unusual. "Carmen? Maybe I should be asking you that question? Is everything okay with Cedric? You?"

"I was hoping you could come over. I really have some-thing to talk to you about, Ms. Eugeena."

"Now? Are you sure you can't wait until tomorrow?"

Carmen hesitated. "I wish I could and I don't want to sound dramatic, but this is really urgent, Ms. Eugeena."

Did she just say urgent? What is going on now, Lord? "Okay. Give me an hour or so, Carmen. I just got back from seeing my aunts and I'm kind of worn out. I will be there as soon as I can. Is Cedric going to be there?"

Carmen was quiet. "No, Cedric is at a conference this week. Thank you, Ms. Eugeena. This means a lot to me. I will see you soon."

At a conference, I thought as I hung up the phone. There was a time when Cedric would have let me know when he was going out of town. I looked over at Porgy, who was peering back at me. "Well, so much for the quiet evening. I can't imagine what Carmen has to share with me especially with Cedric not being home."

Before I went upstairs, I went over to my bag to see who was thinking it was a good idea to call me on my cell phone. I must have not been paying attention to the phone while with Aunt Esther and Cora because I had two messages. I pressed the voicemail. The message was from Pat.

"Ms. Eugeena, I'm so sorry to keep bothering you, but I'm not sure what to think anymore. You know when you have that feeling something isn't right. Well, never mind. If we can meet maybe tomorrow I want to run some things by you."

This was the second time I'd missed Pat's call this week. I wanted to call her back, but I knew Carmen was waiting on me. I'm not sure how I became so popular, but Pat did say we could touch base tomorrow.

It was a shame that Cedric's home was really only ten minutes away from me, but I rarely saw him these days. As I drove, my mind tried to process all the scenarios that Carmen would present me with when I arrived. I imagined she really wanted to get married and wanted to figure out the best way to get Cedric to pop the question. Or what if she was pregnant? Or wanted to move out?

Why am I going over to see this woman again?

Now I really liked Carmen. She was a bit standoffish when I first met her, but I started to see she was a young, intelligent woman who actually did a pretty good job of capturing Cedric's heart and keeping him in line. I just kind of wished I'd raised a young man who wasn't so afraid to commit.

My boys, Junior and Cedric, were quite different in that way. Cedric was the more sensitive of the two and also didn't get along with Ralph. Despite the fact he went into the same profession as his father, delivering babies, the two never did grow close, just tolerated each other.

I took some blame because Ralph and I had quite a distant marriage for many, many years. Going to work and church, raising kids, but somewhere we just went through the motions, often with me picking up the slack of being at football games while Ralph was delivering babies. Prior to Ralph's death we had grown closer, but our marriage had affected each one of our children in a different way.

No one was perfect. You could only do the best you could do.

I turned into the driveway of Cedric and Carmen's townhouse and parked next to Carmen's jeep. She was definitely an interesting mix of a woman. She was a resident at Charleston Hospital, where Cedric was one of the obstetricians on staff. Both were very smart and capable people. Before I could knock or ring the doorbell, the front door was opened by Carmen.

It never failed, but every time I was in Carmen's presence I was struck by her height and beauty. I could see why Cedric was attracted to her. She was just as tall as my son who was over six feet. With looks that rivaled Beyoncé, she was tough girl with a soft, vulnerable side that she had shown on rare occasions in my presence. Her honey-colored hair was cut into a short bob with the left side hanging over her big brown eyes.

"Hey, Ms. Eugeena. I really appreciate you coming by." Carmen held the door open for me.

"Well, you have me intrigued especially since you said Cedric isn't here." I stepped inside the townhouse past Carmen. I hadn't been over to the townhouse since it was Cedric's bachelor pad. As I glanced around, I noticed there was definitely a woman's touch to the place. "It looks nice and cozy in here."

"Thank you, Ms. Eugeena. Do you want anything to drink?"

I was feeling a bit parched. "Water would be good."

"Sure, make yourself at home."

While Carmen disappeared to the back, I decided to stand and continue my examination. Actually, I was trying to take in the fact that the black leather living room set my son had seemed to be gone and replaced by a more refined, but comfortable couch. It was also bright red. That was definitely a reflection of Carmen's personality.

From the looks of the rest of the living room, the fifty-four inch flat screen television was the only toy that Cedric had left from his bachelor days. Or was he still technically a bachelor? *These younguns need to get married and stop playing house. I am too old to be this confused.*

"Here you go, Ms. Eugeena." Carmen handed me a bottle of water. "Why don't you have a seat?"

"Okay." I sat down on the couch, while Carmen sat on the love seat. I twisted off the bottle cap and took a swig of water. Then I waited to see what Carmen had to ask me.

Carmen seemed to be preoccupied with her phone, which was lying on the table.

"Carmen, what did you have to ask me? Everything is okay with Cedric?" I raised my eyebrow. "Is he really at a conference?" I turned my head as if I expected my son to walk out of the back room.

"Yes, he is and I'm sorry." Carmen sighed. "There's a bit of a situation that I was hoping you could help me with."

I eyed Carmen. "Are you pregnant?"

"What? No, I'm not pregnant?"

"Are you sick?"

"Everyone is healthy and there are no problems between me and Cedric. This is about a friend."

"You asked me over for advice for a friend?"

"Yes. Remember I told you a few months ago that I was adopted."

"I remember."

"Well, I found out how to do a search for my biological parents from my friend. She has been doing a search since last year and she's been pretty successful."

"You want my help with searching for your birth parents?"

"I would love if you could help me, but there is something else I was hoping you could help me –"

The doorbell rang interrupting Carmen.

I frowned. "Are you expecting someone else?"

Carmen held up her finger. "Yes, hold just one second."

This was turning out to be a bit of an odd visit, but I was willing to hang. It occurred to me I had a habit of putting people off when I was on my judgmental trip. Leesa liked to remind me of that part of me. I really did like

Carmen and thought she would make a good daughter-in-law. Helping her search for her family could bring us closer.

"Ms. Eugeena, this is my friend."

"What? This is the woman you thought could help me?"

I jumped up from the couch and turned to see Jocelyn Miller walking past Carmen and towards me. Jocelyn was dressed in a bright yellow top with black leggings. Her long curly hair was wrapped in similar yellow scarf.

Lord, help me. I stood my ground thinking, an angry human bumblebee was coming towards me and I needed to get out of the way before I got stung.

Chapter 16

As I held my arms up, two thoughts came to mind one after the other as I stared at Jocelyn. One had to do with that cryptic Facebook post and what had she done so unforgivable. The second thought brought me back to Detective Wilkes' statement. I really didn't know this young woman who stood in front of me with tear-stained eyes and clenched fists.

"Jocelyn, you need to step back, honey. I will defend myself." I stared at Carmen. "What's going on, Carmen? I didn't come over here for this kind of drama."

Carmen sprinted between us and looked from me back to Jocelyn. "You two know each other?"

"We've met," I said. I could feel the heat of Jocelyn's anger as she stared at me. "Are you upset with me?"

Jocelyn screeched. "I should be. If it wasn't for you, I wouldn't have been hauled off my job by the cops."

Well, it certainly didn't take Detective Wilkes long to find Jocelyn.

I felt bad for Jocelyn, but I wasn't the blame. "Excuse me, young lady, before you start making accusations. I didn't tell anyone anything." I put my hand on my hip and pointed towards Jocelyn with the other hand. "You showed up at the nursing home talking about being Louise's granddaughter. Did you not think the staff would be interviewed? Seeing how they have locked down security on visitors, I don't think it was that easy for you to get back there to see Louise without some help."

Jocelyn stared at me a few more seconds before looking away. "You're right. I'm sorry. I did have some help, but she wouldn't have told anyone."

Carmen placed her hand on Jocelyn's shoulder. "Let's calm down. Jocelyn, I didn't know you had already met Ms. Eugeena."

I turned to Carmen. "Exactly what were you trying to do with this meeting? How do you two know each other?"

Carmen sighed. "Why don't we all sit down and I will get us some iced tea."

I sat back down on the couch, while Jocelyn sank into the chair opposite from me. She held her head against the back of the chair and looked at the ceiling.

While Carmen went into the kitchen, I tried to start small talk. "How's your mother?"

Jocelyn focused her eyes on me. "Why would you ask?"

"I'm trying to start a conversation. Carmen asked me here to help. I can leave. I have had a long day. No. A long week. My best friend's life has been turned upside down, and she didn't deserve any of it, much less to be hid away in a nursing home alone now."

Jocelyn looked away. "I'm sorry. I didn't know what happened to Louise's son until they came to get me this morning. It was horrible because I told my mom yesterday how I went to visit Louise. She was furious with me. I was already feeling down about upsetting her. She ranted about how she couldn't forgive me for this one."

I thought back to Jocelyn's Facebook post. "I'm sure your mother understands and will forgive you eventually. Maybe it was a bit much for her at this time."

Carmen arrived back with tall glasses of iced tea. My *maybe* future daughter-in-law did have some hospitality skills. "She sat the tray down on the coffee table. She picked up a glass. "Ms. Eugeena, I have unsweetened tea for you and this is pure honey for you in this bowl if you want to sweeten your tea."

"Thank you, Carmen; I appreciate your thoughtfulness about my diabetes." Once again I questioned why Cedric didn't just pop the question.

Carmen sat down on the couch. "Are you two better now? When Jocelyn told me her story, I really wanted you two to meet each other. Jocelyn, Ms. Louise and Ms. Eugeena have been such great friends for years. I figured she could help with the reunion. Jocelyn's mom was pretty upset. I think Clarice is just scared."

I inquired. "Clarice? Jocelyn, is that your mother's name?"

Jocelyn nodded "Yes. But even if my mom agreed to meet her biological mother, it's ruined now. The cops think I had something to do with killing the woman's son."

I huffed. "Of course you didn't. There was a woman there at the house. I don't know if she was pretending for whatever reason that she wanted to buy the house or William offended her in some way."

Carmen crossed their arms. "The woman could have felt threatened by William. I mean it's not unheard of for people to carry around a weapon. Charleston is not one of the safest cities in the world. Still, if William was trying to sell the house, it seems like he would have been on his best behavior."

I swallowed some of my tea before answering. "That's exactly right. I think the woman came with a plan. I just don't know why. I do know there seemed to be something going on with William when I saw him at the nursing home on Sunday. Junior, my eldest son, saw William a few weeks ago and said he was talking about investing in some technology startup company here in Charleston. It's like he's had this whole lifestyle change." I turned to Jocelyn. "I went by the police station and told Detective Wilkes this same information yesterday."

Jocelyn looked at me. "So you can help prove there was another woman at the house besides me?"

"I don't know how much help I can be. There was a sports car, but it was dark and I only heard a woman's voice. And I know it wasn't your voice even though we've only met one time. My thoughts are the detective should focus on the sudden changes in William's life."

Carmen said, "Ms. Louise might know something."

I shook my head. "There's a lot going on right now with Louise. She's mourning her son and..." I turned to Jocelyn. "I believe your visit set off some memories for her."

"What kind of memories?"

"You wouldn't have happened to have come across information about your maternal grandfather?"

Jocelyn bit her lip. "I didn't, but my mom did. She found out when I was younger about her dad."

"His name was August Manning."

Jocelyn raised her eyebrow. "How did you know? Did Ms. Louise say anything?"

"No, my Aunt Esther did. It seems like your grandfather was one of her students. Interestingly enough, she remembers Louise being around August a few days before his death."

"She remembers? That was fifty years ago."

"Not much gets past Aunt Esther, especially if something made an impact on her. She's pretty sharp despite being in her eighties. What did your mother find?"

"She found members of August's family first. He still has two sisters alive. Thelma and Ruth Manning. They were full of stories about August."

"That's interesting that your mother found her father's side of the family first. How long ago was this?"

"It was about ten years ago. I was still in high school and my dad was alive then. We were all shocked that the sisters lived so close. My dad took my mom to see them. My mom still keeps in touch with them and she insists the sisters come over for Thanksgiving every year."

Ten years ago. "So has your mom reached out to Louise before?"

Jocelyn seemed to warm up and her shoulder slacked as she continued talking. "August's family led us to Louise. You know my mom was never really going to look for her biological parents, but one day she met a woman who turned out to be her cousin. They looked so much alike that the woman insisted my mom had to be related to her. That woman was Ruth's daughter."

I asked, "Were the sisters aware August had a relationship with Louise?"

Jocelyn nodded. "Their mother and my great-grandmother, Sarah Manning, worked for Louise's family. All of them grew up together. Thelma said she knew Louise had gotten pregnant because Louise told her how scared she was if anyone found out. Not too long after August's death, Louise was taken somewhere. The sisters figured she gave the baby up for adoption." Jocelyn's eyes glistened with tears. "They were so overjoyed to see my mom. It was such a letdown when my mom found Louise."

I inquired, "You mean she met Louise and the meeting didn't go well?"

"More like someone stopped her from meeting Louise. There was a man who made it very plain that he didn't want anyone to go near his wife."

I thought back to my earlier conversation with Aunt Esther. Would Bill have been trying to protect his wife or keep her from knowing something he had done? "Jocelyn, you said her husband was the one who stopped your mother from meeting Louise. Did he say why? I mean he didn't leave the window open for her to come back?"

Jocelyn shook her head. "No. In fact my mom said when he saw her at the door; it was like he saw a ghost or something. She didn't really ever tell him that she was Louise's daughter. She just asked if Louise Hopkins was home."

A felt a chill go down my spine. He recognized her, but he'd never seen her before. I thought out loud, "I wondered if Bill recognized August and Louise's features in your mother's face."

"I guess that could be true. My grandfather's sisters said they could even see some of August in me and my brother, especially my brother. I think that's why I was scared when Louise's son showed up on Sunday. I just knew he wasn't going to be there. There was a nurse who was really friendly to me. She told me he didn't come to see her much."

So Jocelyn had been doing some homework. "You talked to Pat before seeing Louise."

"Yes, Pat is her name. I talked to her a few times. When I finally got my nerve up, Pat helped me get into see Mrs. Hopkins on Sunday." Jocelyn twisted her hands like a little girl. "Ms. Eugeena, I had gotten so close to her. I felt like she knew my mother in that photo was her daughter. I saw it in her eyes. You did too. Right, Ms. Eugeena?"

Jocelyn's large eyes were brimming with tears now. I looked at her then over at Carmen, who was just as teary. With Carmen being an adoptee too, I know she was soaking up the conversation and longing to look for her own biological parents.

I nodded to give myself a chance to get my mouth to move. "I believe that Louise would want to get to know you and your mother."

Jocelyn wiped her eyes. "I wanted to set up a meeting for my mom with Louise. She's been down ever since my dad's death. I know meeting her biological mother is still on her mind. My dad tried his best to encourage her to try again before he passed."

Carmen interrupted. "Jocelyn, do you think William would have reacted to you like his father did to your mother? He couldn't have possibly known anything about you or having another sibling? Do you, Ms. Eugeena? I mean it's really very convenient that someone killed him and kind of made sure he was out of the way, if you catch my drift."

Jocelyn turned to Carmen. "Carmen, we've been best friends forever and you know me and my family. None of us would have anything to do with killing William. If anything we would have embraced him as a member of the family."

Carmen grabbed Jocelyn's hands. "Of course not, girl. You know I've been supporting you from day one ever since we found out that Ms. Louise could be your grand-mother. I'm just saying, it's kind of weird."

Carmen turned to me. "I'm sorry, Ms. Eugeena, to catch you off guard like this, but I have been helping Jocelyn get to know Ms. Louise. From what I have found out about Ms. Louise she's never worked, her family was wealthy, owning a plantation back at the turn of the last century. Bill Hopkins was a pretty popular businessman here in Charleston. Sugar Creek isn't upscale, so you couldn't tell it, but I don't believe Louise was hurting for money. I suspect when she died, she probably would have left William a lot of money."

I responded, "It would be hard to tell from the outside that Louise did have money. The Hopkinses enjoyed the simple life and believed in investing money. I don't think their son learned too well how to manage money. Jocelyn, while I don't agree with Detective Wilkes' approach to her investigation, I guess it is smart to look more in the direction of money and who benefits from an inheritance."

Jocelyn yelped. "Well, that just puts this murder on me, like I'm trying to find a way to get to Louise's money. Carmen helped me find out some family history, but I didn't know anything about her money nor do I care. I just wanted to reunite my mother with the one parent she has left."

"I believe you." I assured Jocelyn. I felt like there were a lot more questions that should be asked by the police. Like why did William decide all these years to return to Charleston? I figured when he put his mom in the nursing home, he planned to keep living his nomadic lifestyle, but William clearly had plans to stay in Charleston. By the looks of him prior to his death, William was seeking to live a more upscale lifestyle than what his parents did. What changed and how did those changes lead to his murder?

Chapter 17

I woke up around nine o'clock on Thursday morning, which I thought was pretty late. Being a school teacher with five o' clock in the morning wake-up calls had been my life so long it seemed almost criminal to stay in the bed long past the sun rising. It was a cold morning so for once I had the good sense to snuggle down under the covers and stay put in the bed for a while longer.

Porgy eyed me from his doggy bed. I can't believe I finally broke down and bought the round furry bed, but it was a compromise that allowed him to sleep in the bedroom. The deal was he had his own bed and he was not allowed on mine. "I will get up soon. Can you hang for a few more minutes?"

Porgy lifted his head and barked.

I would not accept anyone telling me that dog didn't know what I was saying.

I took a deep breath as I tried to process yesterday's information overload. I could not stop thinking about young August and young Louise. I know they grew up together, but in that time period, why did they become so careless? I guess I couldn't judge. Young love and naïveté struck mostly everyone as a teenager and when hormones raged at their worst. In this case, the heartache that had been left had everlasting effects for generations.

While I didn't care for William, I couldn't help but feel sorry for him losing his life. He was a spoiled only child and very ungrateful, but his life seemed to be turning around for him before it was cut short. In yesterday's revelations, his murder almost got swept to the side. If William was going to stay in Charleston, I wondered if he was going to take the proceeds from selling his mother's home to buy a more lavish residence.

In his pursuit of living well, where had he slipped up? To me, it felt like William encountered and unknowingly enticed his killer. How and why, I had no clue.

I really needed to see how Louise was doing. I didn't want to be told once again by Ms. Saunders that Louise couldn't accept visitors.

I knew if anyone could tell me Louise's state of mind, Pat could tell me what was really going on. Plus I knew Pat wanted to tell me something? I should have returned her messages from both Monday and Wednesday, but so much had happened.

When I called Pat her phone rang and rang, but never went to voicemail. *Mmm, that's weird.* I would try again later. Maybe we could finally stop playing phone tag with each other.

With that thought, I climbed out of the bed with Porgy yapping at my feet. After finally getting dressed, I decided to do something I had put off for at least two weeks now. When the cold weather came in I stopped my morning walk. I decided to snap a leash on Porgy and for a change we would walk. The morning's fall air was brisk, requiring the need for a jacket, but the sun was bright in the sky. Porgy was a little thing, but he had a bit of strength on him as he pulled me along towards the sidewalk.

I'm not sure if Porgy was reading my mind, but we didn't get too far before we stopped, right in front of Louise's house. The yellow crime scene tape was still around the front door. If I could have snuck a peek in the house, I would have. Instead I walked over to where William's car sat, now without its owner. As I moved closer, I noticed that there were temporary plates on the car. William had purchased this car less than three weeks ago. The new purchase didn't startle me as much as the car dealership name.

Chuck Nelson Buick of Charleston.

Chuck Nelson. That was one of the names Aunt Esther mentioned yesterday. Now that I thought of it, one of the most annoying local commercials was who I believed was Chuck Nelson's son looking as shady as a salesman could look spouting all the deals he had for those looking for a car. *Credit or no credit.*

Porgy didn't seem bothered that I was preoccupied with the car and nosed his way in the grass next to it. I leaned over and peeked into the car.

Since William's father and Chuck Nelson were really good friends, I wondered if William received some type of deal on this car. It was very nice and luxurious, not at all like the pickup trucks I've seen William driving over the years.

I had discovered some interesting aspects to Louise's life, but her deceased son was a character all his own. I looked at the back of the car and realized there were tire tracks in the driveway.

I bet that sports car left those tire tracks when its owner

wheeled out of the driveway on Sunday. I bent down like I was some forensic scientist to study the tracks closer. Surely the detective had this as a clue. From what I've seen on TV they can match these down to the types of tires that can be found on vehicles.

"Eugeena, what are you up to? Are you okay?"

I straightened up and almost screamed. I placed my hands on my chest to hopefully calm my heart. "Good morning, Amos. I didn't hear you walking up behind me?"

Amos was dressed with a jacket, which I figured was over a pair of overalls. He did, at least, seem to have a variety of overalls. These were dark gray. He raised an eyebrow. "I would imagine not. If you're going to be snooping, you should also remain alert."

"Snooping? Oh you don't know the half of what I found out yet and I can tell you I haven't been snooping. People have been dropping information on me without me even having to ask for it."

"You don't say? I thought you were going to let the police handle it."

"Well, who's to say—," Porgy for some reason decided to run around my legs at that moment. I grabbed the leash before he totally tied me up. "Come here, little dog. You and I don't need to be tangled." After I managed to get the leash from around my legs, I looked at Amos. "You may not believe me, but I tried my best to stay out of this little situation, but it has grown over the past two days. I'm thinking the good Lord must want me to know something because people are seeking me out with information."

Amos laughed. "Is that so?"

I walked around to the back of the car and looked back at the temporary plate. "You see this name on this plate."

Amos eyed me. "Chuck Nelson."

"Keep that name in your mind, because after I tell you what all I've found out, your mind is going to be as blown as mine. Right now, I need two of us on this. You had breakfast yet? If not, I will clue you in."

A few moments later, I had cheese grits bubbling on the stove. I have always been a lover of cheese though I've changed my eating habits. This morning felt like as good a time as any to eat comfort food. By the time I finished talking; Amos sat looking wide-eyed over his empty bowl.

"Wow! You're not kidding. You basically dug up a cold case."

"You're right. But does one murder really have to do anything with the other murder?"

"I don't think so. I'm pretty sure the only connection there is this Jocelyn Miller and her mother."

"I kind of agree with you, but it's almost like Jocelyn showing up has pulled back secrets that have been hidden for many years. I can see why Detective Wilkes wants to start by looking at Jocelyn, but my concern is William. I've never seen him driving a brand new car like that. Him walking around dressed like something out of Esquire is highly suspicious to me."

"I agree with you on that. Detective work is pretty tricky. You definitely need to focus on the victim and track their timeframe, but then we always want to understand what would motivate someone to kill. Finding the motive is high on Detective Wilkes' priority list."

"I'm still not seeing how she is finding any motive. Even if Louise was to accept her long lost daughter and her family, she would have been able to provide William and her daughter with money. Louise may look homely when she wants to, but she was and has always been well off financially."

"Not everyone sees it that way. When you have been in the business of solving crimes you're trained to see people at their worst. Sometimes it's smarter to think of what's the worst a person could do rather than thinking what's not possible. Anyone can commit a crime when pushed by their circumstances. Do you know how well off Jocelyn's mother is right now? Why is Jocelyn looking now?"

I waved at Amos. "Okay, okay, I see your point. I've talked to Jocelyn and I believe she's sincere or a really good actress. Plus, Jocelyn drives a bright red car. It looked nothing like that car, what you say could have been a Mustang. Can't Detective Wilkes have those tire threads tracked?"

Amos shook his head. "My, my woman, maybe you ought to have been a detective because you certainly have been bitten by the bug."

"I'm just naturally curious. I really felt bad for Jocelyn last night. I'm sensitive that time is being wasted in the wrong direction."

"Speaking of time, have you had time to talk to Louise?"

I shook my head. "I haven't and I want to, but it appears she's hasn't been handling William's death very well. At least that's what the Hillcrest Manor director told me."

I smiled as another thought started to creep in. "You wouldn't be too busy this afternoon, Amos? I kind of like that car that William purchased."

Amos eyed me and then a slow grin stretched across his face. "Nope. I don't have anything planned at all."

Now that put a smile on my face. I may have been bitten by this detective stuff, but I had sense enough to call on an experienced detective to help me.

I certainly couldn't have asked for a better partner in crime.

Chapter 18

Amos talked me into getting a good night's sleep and heading over to Chuck Nelson's dealership mid-morning on Friday. I couldn't believe it was already the end of the week.

Amos decided he would drive us to the dealership, which suited me just fine. I didn't often get to be a passenger. Unfortunately, I had to catch myself from admiring Amos' side profile long enough to remember to confirm with him what we were doing. "Tell me the truth, are you sure you don't think this is silly idea? I mean you're just coming so I won't get myself into trouble, aren't you?"

Amos raised an eyebrow. "If I didn't come with you, you would have found a way to get out here and ask questions. That got you in trouble this past summer. Are you having second thoughts now?"

I shook my head. "No. I'm really interested in finding out if this James Nelson was close friends with William since their fathers were friends."

Amos nodded. "Let me guess, I bet you really want

access to James' father, Chuck Nelson, to ask about a crime that happened fifty years ago."

"I'm not expecting a confession from a man in his seventies, but I would love to see his face to see if there's a hint of guilt."

Amos reminded, "Let's concentrate on what we can gather now. Remember, we're not here to investigate a cold case. Peace to August Manning's soul, but we do want to find out information about William."

I wasn't sure what we would find, but Amos thought it was best for us to start a conversation under the illusion of purchasing a car. Apparently, I wasn't the only one seeking adventure as a retiree. Amos has been retired at least a year before me, and I've always wondered if he just spent his time in the yard or fiddling around with woodwork in his shack.

As Amos pulled into the parking lot, I noticed there were two men standing outside talking. I suspected they were both salesmen since they were dressed in suits. I'm pretty sure I wasn't imagining the look in their eyes. They were primed and ready to pounce on new prey.

After Amos parked his car, I hesitated for a moment before opening the door. I wanted to observe the salesmen from the passenger mirror. One of the men had already started walking towards to us. "This is going to be interesting."

Amos grinned. "Let's see if they can talk us into buying a car." He climbed out of the driver's side.

"Mmm. I'm fine with my car." I opened the car door and stepped out very slow. I haven't been to a car dealership in a decade. I went with Ralph to purchase a car with only intentions of picking out the color and features I wanted. My Toyota Camry was at 200,000 miles, but it remained in good condition due to my continuing to stick to a car maintenance schedule after Ralph's death.

As the salesman drew closer, I recognized his face and was very much convinced God had set up this divine meeting. James Nelson walked purposely towards us with his hand wrapped around his red tie as if he wanted to keep it from flying back in his face.

I commented to Amos. "He looks just the way he looks on those commercials."

Amos crossed his arms. "How else should he look, Eugeena?"

"I don't know. I was expecting him to be a lot taller."

Amos grunted something.

James approached us with a grin that revealed straight white teeth that had to come from braces. The way he stretched his mouth reminded me of a clown's mouth without all the makeup. "Howdy folks, are you here look-ing for a brand new car? We have quite the special going on now." He stretched his arm to guide our eyes across the parking lot. "The special has been going on all month. Great deal because we need to move all of these cars by the end of the year."

I wondered if William received the special when he purchased his car a few weeks ago.

James held out his hand like he was escorting us on a grand tour. "Shall I show you and your husband around?"

I don't know who started coughing first. It was like something was in the air giving me a coughing fit and Amos too. I wanted to correct the salesman, but he'd already started walking. I looked over at Amos who shrugged and followed the salesman.

What? Isn't Amos going to correct him?

For those next few minutes, we covered the parking lot

before we stopped in front of a row of Buick Lacrosses. I did see why William liked the car, although it still felt like a departure from his usual vehicles over the years.

James beamed. "So folks what do you think of this Lacrosse? It's a beauty isn't it?"

Amos answered, "Looks like a winner."

I was ready to move this conversation along. "Can we take a test drive?"

I thought to myself if James smiled any harder, his jaw-bone would shatter. "I will get the keys."

Amos was looking at me with one eyebrow raised. "A test drive? We didn't talk about that, Eugeena."

I shrugged. "How else are we supposed to ask questions? You do the driving."

Amos started to protest, but I stopped him.

"You assured me neither one of us will be leaving this parking lot with a car payment." I winked at him and turned away to see James bounding back towards us.

He asked, "Are you ready to take this baby for a spin?"

"Sure, let's do this." Amos took the keys and climbed into the driver's seat, while I opened the back door and sat in the back.

James asked, "Ma'am, are you sure you don't want to sit up front with your husband?"

I closed the back door and then snapped my seatbelt in place. I peered at James. "He's
not my husband."

"Oh." James's smile faltered a bit, but kept looking cheerful as he glanced back and forth from me to Amos.

Amos started the car. "Let's go. Mr. Nelson, we're waiting on you."

"Yes, sure." James jumped in the passenger seat. "Let's take a right at the end of the driveway."

Amos maneuvered the steering wheel, guiding us out of the parking lot. I thought Amos looked like he enjoyed the car.

"So, uh, folks what made you interested in this car?" James asked.

Bingo. I spoke up for the back seat. "I actually told Amos about the car. My neighbor has one of these cars. Or I should say he had one like it."

James turned around, appearing puzzled. "Did you say had? He got rid of it for another car?"

"Oh no. He just isn't able to drive the car anymore."

James looked at Amos and then back at me. "Accident?"

I shrugged. "He died."

"Oh."

Thank goodness, the man finally dropped that crazy grin.

I leaned forward as much as the back seatbelt would let me. "I was admiring his car and noticed he bought it from your dealership maybe two weeks ago. I would have never imagined William driving such a luxurious car."

Amos peered at me via the rearview mirror. His eyes held questions as to where I was going with the questions.

James seemed to be interested. "Did you say your friend's name was William?"

I responded, "He wasn't so much a friend. Now his mother is a dear friend of mine. Do you know Louise Hopkins?"

James seemed lost for words. He recovered and told Amos, "Why don't you take the exit to I-26. You will find this ride is real smooth on the highway."

I had to give James credit for keeping in salesman

mode, although I could tell he was disturbed that I brought up William.

"Mr. Nelson, did you know William? I'm sorry if you didn't know he died."

James loosened the tie's knot. "I heard. Yes, William and I grew up together. It's very sad to hear what happened to him."

I decided to keep talking, not really sure why, but there was no need to waste the test drive as Amos eased down the ramp into I-26 traffic. "It's a shame. William was really getting his head together, investing in some startup company here in Charleston, buying a luxury car and the last time I saw him, he looked like some GQ model. I just feel so bad for his mother, you know with him being her only child."

James looked over his shoulder. "I feel bad for him too. He was here a few weeks ago. I hadn't seen him that excited about being in Charleston in a long time. He talked about finally doing something to make his dad proud."

I asked, "Was he talking about his company? I never imagined William was the business type."

James rubbed his hands through his hair. "He wasn't. I told him to slow it down and be sure he really studied his investment."

James spoke to Amos. "Sorry we got off topic there. How do you like the car? You can take that exit so we can head back and talk more."

Amos nodded.

I wanted to continue to ride. I had a lot more questions. "Do you know what kind of company? I didn't know we had so many technology companies here in Charleston?"

James's smile returned, "Oh, yes, Charleston is one of the top ten fastest growing cities for software and technology companies. William told me his company was developing healthcare apps. You know, they are all the new rage now."

Really? That was interesting and also the last type of business I expected William to be involved in.

Amos drove us back to the parking lot and stopped in front of the door.

I asked James, "So, William was planning to stay in Charleston? I wondered why he was selling his mother's house."

"The Charleston Digital Corridor is a big draw here for tech companies. I believe he preferred staying downtown. He was staying in one of those fancy hotels. The Belmont, I think."

After we all climbed out of the car, James plastered on that huge smile and asked Amos, "So what do you think?"

I answered, "That William sure hit pay dirt."

James' smile slipped from his face. "I was talking about the car. But you're right, I guess he did. Funny how he struck it rich. Of course, I've always heard his mother came from money. At least that's what my dad used to say."

Amos grabbed my elbow. "Thanks for the test drive. That sure is a nice car. I think I will sleep on it. Eugeena, we should head back."

James almost whined. "Wait, you liked the car, right? I'm sure I can work out a deal for you."

Amos was guiding me back towards his car, but I still had a few questions. I turned around. "You know you said you grew up with William. So you knew Bill Hopkins? I mean your families are friends."

James frowned. "My dad and William's dad grew up together. He was actually closer to William's mom. I believe if Bill Hopkins hadn't married her, my dad would have. Of course, I'm glad he didn't or I and my siblings wouldn't be here. That would be a shame."

Louise and Chuck. "That's so interesting. How's Chuck Nelson doing these days, I mean with his son running the business?"

He glanced at me briefly. I believe I saw bit of annoyance flash in his eyes. It could have been because he had his salesman eyes on new prey. A much younger couple, probably married, was walking towards us and appeared to have money to spend. I sensed James didn't really want to talk about his dad, but he answered.

"My dad's not doing too well these days. Alzheimer's. It was really nice chatting with you folks. Mr. Jones, here's my card. I hope to hear from you soon." With a wink, James plastered on that megawatt smile and took off across the parking lot.

Amos opened the passenger car door for me. I couldn't wait until he went around to the driver's side and climbed in. I commented, "What do you think? This is quite the triangle or circle. There's Bill and Louise. August and Louise. Now Chuck and Louise. I've seen photos of Louise when she was younger and I know she was quite a pretty woman, but who would have guessed she had it going on like that?"

Amos nodded. "Sounds like August was her first love, but he lost out worse than the other two."

I shook my head. "I'm not seeing Bill being one to hurt August, but then again Jocelyn said he was the one who ran her mother away from seeing Louise."

"He could have been trying to protect Louise."

"From what? How did Bill win Louise over instead of Chuck?"

Now that I thought back to past conversations with Louise, she told me she married Bill because he was familiar and a comfort to her after her disastrous first marriage. They were all in their early twenties. It was possible Chuck was already married, but I wondered how he let Louise get away. How did Bill and Chuck manage to remain friends when both men had an interest in Louise?

I believe August ultimately won Louise's heart first, which made his death even more tragic.

Chapter 19

I was really concerned about Louise. I certainly wanted to know more about this Chuck Nelson. Did Louise know she was, essentially, in the middle of a love triangle? But only one had lost his life. Between Bill and Chuck, could one of them or both have been responsible for August's murder?

Instead of calling, I decided to drive to Hillcrest Manor Nursing Home first thing Saturday morning. To my chagrin, the young woman who was at the desk last Sunday watched me carefully as I approached. I hoped Pat would show up like she did the last time. As I approached the desk, I tried to ease into a conversation. "Hello, how are you? It's Lexi, right? Do you remember me?"

Lexi looked around me like she'd become uncomfortable and was seeking help.

I decided to cut to the chase before the little woman decided to locate security. I mean I wasn't any kind of threat. I just wanted to check on my friend. "Is Pat here?"

Lexi said sharply, "Pat no longer works here."

I opened my mouth and shut it quickly. "You must not

be talking about Patricia Brown known to me as Pat. Pat has been working at the nursing home for five years. She loves working in this place."

Lexi shrugged as if she couldn't care less. "I only know that she hasn't showed up to work since Wednesday, so I assumed she quit."

Wednesday. I wondered if Pat had gotten sick. "Are you sure? I mean flu season is here. Surely she called in sick."

"No." Lexi shook her head. "She said something to upset the director. They were arguing here just the other day."

Now that I thought back to Monday, Pat was having words with Ms. Saunders. Pat could be a hot head, but she wouldn't have done anything to jeopardize her job unless there was something that really had her upset. I knew this woman. After getting clean from her heroin addiction, Pat had worked diligently to obtain her nursing license and she especially wanted to work with geriatrics.

What I did know was Pat rarely missed church service. I would grab her after church on Sunday to get the real deal.

Lexi's high-pitched voice broke into my thoughts. "If you're here trying to see Mrs. Hopkins, I'm sorry we can't allow you to see her."

"Allow. I've been visiting her every week since July. I know she's grieving her son, please know I understand and only want to do what I can to help."

Lexi responded, "It's more than that, Mrs. Patterson. Mr. Hopkins no longer wanted you to see his mother."

My mouth dropped. "Are you kidding me? Mr. Hopkins is deceased. I was here on Monday to help deliver the bad news."

"I have to follow the rules. You can speak to the director."

"I certainly will. William and I didn't always see eye to eye, but he was not *that* against me visiting his mother."

Lexi sighed deeply as though I was annoying her. "I'm really sorry."

I got the feeling she wasn't sorry at all. I frowned, "Lexi, why did Ms. Saunders make all of these rules for visitors?"

"I guess when we let a criminal into the place."

I sucked in my breath. "What criminal?"

Lexi shrugged, "That young woman who came to visit Mrs. Hopkins on Sunday. I heard the police questioned her about shooting Mr. Hopkins. I knew something wasn't right about her."

I leaned forward. "What do you mean?"

Lexi looked up at me wide-eyed. "She's been here sneaking around and talking to other patients."

"Other patients? Who?"

Lexi looked past me. "You really need to go now."

I turned to find Ms. Saunders looking at me from down a hallway. I was really confused so I just whirled around and walked out. Why did it feel like I was being treated like a criminal? I really needed to find Pat. My head was spinning and I couldn't focus on one single thought by the time I reached my car. After I sat down and closed the car door, what really bothered me was Lexi's statement about Jocelyn. Detective Wilkes was low-key and very cautious with her investigations. Jocelyn admitted it took her some time to get up the nerve and it sounded like Pat had helped her get in to see Louise. Were the rules really created because Jocelyn was looking suspicious?

I started my car and decided it was time to do my favorite activity. A few minutes later I pulled into the Food

Lion parking lot. Something about pushing a shopping cart up and down the aisle was still calming. Now, my grocery store visits in the past resulted in me filling the shopping cart with items I had no business eating. My Type 2 diabetes has since sobered me.

Like every other time I enter the grocery store, I map out in my head to look past the sweets in the deli section and purposely turn my head towards the fruit. Apples have always been a favorite and not just because they're symbolic of education, but munching on an apple truly did calm my nerves. That's what I needed.

I took my time and picked out some Red Delicious apples and then a few Granny Smith apples. I twisted the bags and placed them in my cart, feeling pretty good about my safe start until I turned to see a display of cakes.

Why did they have to put the apples so close to the deli sweets?

Then a thought came to mind. I'd almost forgotten.

Okay I hadn't forgotten, I just quietly tucked it into the back of my mind that my birthday was the next Wednesday. I wasn't planning on a big celebration. Approaching sixty was in itself a major feat, but I didn't need to celebrate another whole decade of life with a group of people. I could treat myself to one of those cakes.

No, Eugeena! I turned away from the cake as visions of fluffy yellow moist cake covered in creamy vanilla icing sent my senses in another direction.

I pushed the cart forward, my mind apparently still on the cake behind me not realizing a cart was in front of me. I cringed as I banged into the shopping cart sending it forward about four feet.

"Eugeena, is that you?"

A split second later, I heard another voice.

"Yep, that's her."

I froze in my steps because I really didn't need to run into those two. After what I'd just heard about Pat, you have to take some chance encounters as God-destined. So I sucked up my discomfort and turned to find the Brown twins staring at me.

Double trouble for sure even though Annie Mae and Willie Mae Brown looked cute in their matching navy blue sweat suits. Even after all these years that I've known them, it was hard to tell the two sisters apart sometimes. I blinked and waited.

Annie Mae's wandering eye was often a clue. She never disappointed. I couldn't tell if she was staring at me or the vegetables behind me.

Willie Mae who claimed to be the oldest by a minute, usually looked younger than Annie Mae, but today I detected that extra minute had caught up with her. I smiled. "How are you ladies doing today?"

Annie Mae replied, "We're fine. How are you feeling, Eugeena?" She walked towards the cart that had been pushed by me.

Great! That would be their shopping cart.

Willie Mae stepped closer and asked, "Yes. We heard what happened to your neighbor? It's not going too well in your neighborhood now?"

Annie Mae rolled the runaway cart closer. "Didn't Sugar Creek used to be safer? I mean didn't poor Mary just get killed in her own home a few months ago."

My head went back and forth from one twin to the other as they slung questions at me. I blinked to recover from the whiplash my neck just undertook. "Yes, it's been a bit different."

Willie Mae looked over in my cart. "You're just eating

apples. I hope you're going to buy more food than that. Although, you have been losing weight."

Annie Mae made a point of looking inside my cart too.

She commented, "If you add carrots and lettuce, Eugeena, you will be eating just like a rabbit."

Did these women not know I just walked into the store before they started harassing me? I had several more aisles to cover. "Ladies, I'm so glad you noticed I slimmed down. Losing all that weight has made managing my sugar much easier."

Annie Mae grinned. "Oh yeah, that's right. Girl, I'm glad I'm as healthy as a horse at my age." Annie stepped closer until she was right beside me. "Speaking of sugar, Mr. Jones must like your new look too."

I blinked again, thinking I never remembered getting this much attention when Ralph was alive. I guessed because the man I was hanging around wasn't Ralph.

Annie Mae placed her hand on her chest. "Oh, I'm sorry! That's none of my business what goes on between you and Mr. Jones. We just thought you two were an item since you sit next to each other at church sometimes."

It was time to change the conversation. I turned away from Annie Mae and looked at Willie Mae who seemed quieter than usual. "Have you seen, Pat? When I went by the nursing home a while ago I was told Pat had quit. I thought that couldn't be true."

I watched the look that passed between the twins. The look struck me because it was the first time I think I ever saw genuine worry on either of their faces. They always seemed to be in competition for who could be the better ice queen.

Something is not right.

Pat was Willie Mae's only child. Since Annie Mae

never had children, she considered Pat just as much her daughter too. Both women could be hell-raisers, but I personally witnessed them pray and intervene for Pat's life years ago while she struggled to get clean from heroin.

Willie Mae exclaimed, "My Pat didn't quit. Who said that? She, she..." Willie Mae put her hands to her face and started shaking.

Oh no! I turned and looked around us. I was not expecting Willie Mae to start crying in the middle of the grocery store aisle between the apples and oranges. The twins were not known for displaying emotion and certainly not in public. My heart began to race. "I'm sorry, Willie Mae. I didn't mean to upset you."

Annie Mae came around and patted her sister on the shoulder. "It's going to be okay, Sister. Eugeena, we haven't seen Pat since Thursday morning. Willie Mae and Pat had a bit of an argument. We tried to calm her down, but she just left. This isn't like her not to show up." Annie Mae seemed to struggle with her own emotions. "At least it has been a while since she's done this. She's been a really good girl."

Pat was almost forty years old, but I knew what Annie Mae meant. Pat was still their little girl and they were afraid something sent Pat off the wagon after all these years.

I looked around as other shoppers were peering at us. I didn't care about the onlookers, but was clearly disturbed that Pat seemed to be missing. The last time I saw Pat was the Monday when we broke the news to Louise about William's death. She'd also left that voicemail. I tried to call her. "Do you mind me asking what Pat was upset about?"

Annie Mae pulled out some crumbled tissues and

spread one out to hand to her sister. Willie Mae took it and blew her nose. "She was really upset about something at work. I think she argued with her boss about something. I told her that wasn't a good idea."

"Well, it's been over forty-eight hours have you told the police?"

Annie Mae rolled her eyes. "Of course we did, Eugeena. They told us she was an adult and after they heard that Willie Mae and Pat had a fight, they really thought she just wanted to get away."

This sounded way too familiar. It was hard to get the police to take it seriously when an adult took off sometimes, especially if they had a drug addiction history like Pat. I had a similar problem when Leesa ran off earlier this summer, dumping my two grandchildren practically in my lap. "You have no idea what the argument was about with her boss?"

Willie Mae heaved her chest and stuttered. "Something about changes on her job. She felt like some of the patients were being mistreated."

Louise. Was that what Pat wanted to talk to me about?

I commented out loud to the twins. "I have been noticing something different in the past few weeks at the nursing home. I used to be able to walk in and talk to Louise, now they're taking great care in checking out who's coming to visit. On Sunday, the only way I saw Louise was with Pat's help."

Now I was starting to wonder if William would not have really wanted me to visit his mother. If he didn't, he would have stopped me from the very beginning. It wasn't like he was taking time out to come visit her. In fact, I had a feeling that William would have been happy if Louise slipped away and left him to live his life with her money.

But something went wrong. William was gone.

Was Pat a casualty too? *Why?* Nothing was making sense to me.

Chapter 20

After I arrived home and put my groceries in the refrigerator, I called Amos. I could've called anyone else, but I knew Amos would set my nerves back right. Unfortunately, he didn't answer so I busied myself by doing my usual Saturday afternoon activities. I cleaned the house a bit more than usual since I had Porgy around.

All the while I vacuumed I thought about Pat and what could've upset her. Pat talked to William when he came to visit Louise, just hours before his death. The next day, I noticed Pat having an animated conversation with Ms. Saunders. Being a nurse, Pat saw to the most intimate details about her patients. Was she showing concern about Louise's welfare in the wake of William's death or was there something else bothering Pat? Did the new director think Pat speaking up was not a good thing?

I guess realistically I could see Pat quitting out of frustration if she was not receiving support. I knew Pat was about getting to the truth. She wouldn't abandon or leave an issue alone. I truly hope she was somewhere thinking about what to do and would reach out to me again. It was the part about never hearing from her that had been worrying me all afternoon. I knew worrying didn't do a bit of good, but I'd had uneasiness in my spirit for a whole week. It was hard to shake.

After I cleaned to my heart's content, I curled up on my couch with my bible. The next day would be Sunday so I turned my thoughts to reviewing the Sunday School lesson. The reading was from a familiar passage in Acts chapter nine where Paul, known originally as Saul, was knocked down blind on his way to Damascus. The funny thing was Saul was on his way to persecute followers of Jesus and Jesus stopped him cold on his journey. I'd always liked reading the book of Acts and seeing how God could turn anyone around.

The lessons reminded me of Pat's turn around over the past seven years from heroin addict to caring nurse. I was a bit ashamed, but I hadn't thought about whether or not William had also gone through a life changing experience. The way he came back in town and placed Louise in the nursing home, I had my doubts. Though he appeared to look handsome and put together on the outside, I couldn't be too sure what was going on the inside.

Before heading to bed, I tried calling Amos again. It occurred to me if Louise was still next door and something was on her mind, she would've been calling me and vice versa.

"Hello, Eugeena?"

"Now how did you know it was me?"

"Caller ID."

"Oh." *I knew that.*

"Is everything okay?"

"Yes and no." I filled Amos in on my Saturday and then waited for his comments.

"Don't worry about, Pat. She probably needed to blow off steam. You need to be taking care of yourself. This week has been challenging for you."

"Amos, I don't think I've ever felt this helpless."

"I'm going to tell you something my wife used to tell me."

That made me curious. "Okay?"

"Let God handle it."

I had to smile. One because Amos had given me the very advice I needed to hear. With both of us being widowed, we only on certain occasions brought up our deceased spouses. I asked, "Did you listen to her advice, Amos?"

He chuckled. "Most of the time I didn't and I have a feeling you may be just as hard-headed." His voice turned serious. "Believe me, you will drive yourself crazy trying to figure out people. I had too many cases that really drove me to wonder about the human race. It can be depressing."

"You're not kidding and as a former detective, I know you know more than anybody. Are you going to church in the morning?"

"No. I have something that I need to take care of tomorrow."

"Oh."

"Don't you worry about it. You get some rest, Eugeena. Answers will come when it's time."

"I know you're right. Goodnight, Amos."

"Goodnight, Eugeena."

I felt a bit better. But I knew what would really help me sleep. I sank to my knees and prayed specifically for protection for Pat. *Lord, you know what Pat has been through and you know her heart. Please bring her back safely to us.*

On Sunday morning when I stepped inside Missionary

Baptist Church, I immediately noticed the Brown sisters were missing. It was almost ten o'clock. Since the twins had a key, they often opened the church doors making them the first arrivals at church each Sunday. No one owned a church, but Willie Mae and Annie Mae pretty much kept reign over most of the church boards including the usher board. I really expected them to greet me in their own special way when I entered the vestibule.

I walked down the aisle of the sanctuary, thinking it was so quiet without the twins chattering on about a non-issue from the back of the church. When I reached the middle of the aisle, I heard my name. I turned to see Pastor George Jones walking toward me.

Like most of the younger people at church, I'd watched Pastor Jones grow up under the leadership of our previous pastor and his father, Tennessee Jones. Pastor Jones wiped his brow with a handkerchief before asking, "Sister Eugeena, how are you this morning?"

"Not too good, Pastor. Have you heard from the Browns?"

Pastor Jones was tall and massive in size. While he appeared calm, I noticed his eyes were not. He didn't look directly at me. "I talked to Sister Annie Mae this morning. Sister Willie Mae isn't doing too well. You know I've never known either sister to be sick."

I exclaimed, "Well I can't blame them. They're worried sick about Sister Pat."

"I know, it's upsetting, but I told them it's only been a few days. We can only pray that Pat will return safely. Now I have a favor to ask of you. Since Sister Pat isn't here, would you mind taking over her Sunday School class this morning?"

I hesitated for just a moment because I knew Pat taught

the middle school class. I looked at the pastor. "If that's what you need me to do."

Pastor Jones patted my shoulder. "I know you're the best one for the job. Thank you, Sister Eugeena."

I was glad I reviewed the Sunday School lesson. When I entered the classroom, there were only five students in Pat's Sunday School class and they all stared at me as though I was some alien. A young woman who wore her hair in braids asked, "Is Ms. Pat going to be here today?"

The sadness in her face dampened my spirits just a little. I swallowed, "Not today, honey, but we're going to have some fun like Ms. Pat would want us too."

Sunday School passed quickly and I enjoyed being around the teens although I could tell they missed Pat. That spoke volumes to me about the kind of person Pat was if the young people were looking forward to her teaching.

Not seeing the twins sitting in their special corner, where no one else dared to sit was a little unsettling. Despite the missing Brown family, I appreciated Pastor Jones' word, "Do not despair." *We are troubled on every side, yet not distressed; we are perplexed, but not in despair. 2 Corinthians 4:8*

After I arrived home, I changed out of my church clothes and then picked up the phone. I had to know what was going on with the Browns.

"Hello. Pat?" Willie Mae sounded worn down and as if she anticipated hearing her daughter's voice instead of mine.

I was so sorry to disappoint. "Willie Mae, it's Eugeena. I noticed you and Annie Mae were missing from church today. No word on Pat?"

Willie Mae sighed deeply into the phone. "No, I'm

afraid not." Willie was quiet for a second, before continuing. "Annie thinks she's regressed."

"Pat was disappointed about the way things were going with her job, but your daughter was not willing to go back to drugs. She really cared for her patients."

"I know," Willie Mae sniffled. "When I woke up the next morning and realized Pat had not come back home, I knew I shouldn't have argued with her. I should have listened to her."

"Willie Mae, Pat left me some voicemails. I never got a chance to ever get back in touch with her. I think Pat was trying to tell me something about the nursing home and Louise. Is it possible that Pat gave you a hint about what was bothering her?"

Willie Mae said, "She told me the new director had fired some of the nurses, really accusing people of things they had not done. Pat was afraid she was next because she was always speaking her mind. I told her she needed to keep her mouth closed."

I really wished I could have heard the conversation Pat had with Ms. Saunders. *What did Pat have on her mind?* I tuned back into Willie Mae and realized I missed something she had said. "Willie Mae, did you just say Pat left to go somewhere on Thursday. Where was she going?"

"I believe she was going back to the nursing home."

"This was on Thursday when you last saw her. At what time?"

"She left before noon, I think."

That was strange. When I talked to that Lexi girl, she'd said Pat hadn't been back to work since Wednesday. So did Pat ever make it to the nursing home on Thursday after arguing with her mother?

I wanted to question Willie Mae more, but my front

doorbell rang. I looked at the clock. Who was that? My first thought was Amos, but since he was so mysterious about what he was up to I figured we were skipping Sunday dinner today.

"Willie Mae, someone is at my door. You and Annie Mae don't worry. Pat will be fine and we're going to get down to the bottom of what's going on at that nursing home."

I said goodbye to Willie Mae and shuffled over to the door.

When I peeked through the peep hole, I can say I was pleased to see the tall, lanky young man at the door. It had been some time since I've had a surprise visit from him.

Chapter 21

Cedric Patterson peered at me over his gold wire-framed glasses, looking very much like his father. My middle child was once awkward and skinny for the longest until he seemed to morph into the handsome man that now stood before me. Cedric had always been more of a ladies' man than I would have liked, but he was also a well-respected doctor who delivered babies.

I eyed my missing-in-action son. "So what brings you here, stranger? You used to just come in when you wanted to. When did you finally learn to start ringing the doorbell?" I crossed my arms. "Let me guess. You forgot your keys."

Cedric grinned. "We're all adults, Mama. I don't need to be barging in on you. Besides, I thought you might have company." He stepped inside and reached down to pet Porgy who was running around in circles.

I closed the door and called to Porgy, "Calm down, doggie." It amazed me how that dog remembered everyone. "What do you mean by company? It's just me and Porgy. Have you and Junior been talking?"

He strode into the living room over to what had to be the most popular chair in the living room, with Porgy right on his heels. "Sources have reported you and Mr. Amos have been spending many Sunday dinners together."

I rolled my eyes. "Sounds *like* that source would be your sister, who along with her children, were well fed last week."

Cedric sat down in his father's chair. "She might have mentioned something about being here last weekend. I also heard William was killed."

I sat down across from him on the couch. Porgy sat by my feet, keeping his eyes on Cedric. "It sounds like you've gotten pretty caught up despite being out of town for a weeklong conference."

Cedric looked away. "I'm sorry; I probably should have mentioned that to you."

"You're a grown man, Cedric. You don't need to tell me anything."

"It looks like I should be checking on you more. By the way, Carmen told me you came by the place to help her with a friend, Jocelyn. I appreciate you helping Carmen."

"I like Carmen." I raised my eyebrow. "She really would be a great daughter-in-law too, on a more official basis."

Cedric's caramel skin had a rosy glow creeping up around his ears, appearing as though I caught him in the act of doing something he wasn't supposed too. "I have missed talking to you. You have a birthday coming up soon."

I loved how my son subtly changed the subject. "Yes. Wednesday."

"Any plans?"

"Nope. A nice quiet birthday works for me." I watched

Cedric rub his hands across the top of his head. "Did you come to ask about my birthday or was there something else on your mind, son?"

He laughed and then stood. "That's why I miss talking to you, Mama. I can never really hide anything from you. You could always tell when something is up." He stopped. "Carmen is like that too. I can't hide anything from her."

"She has good instincts and I can tell she's in tune with you."

Cedric started to pace. The eeriness of his pacing was too similar to when his father, Ralph, would do the same thing in that almost very spot.

I had to ask, "Cedric, you and Carmen have only been living together a few months. Are you having second thoughts?"

Cedric stopped pacing and turned to look at me. "I am having second thoughts, but not about what you think?"

"Okay. Cedric, you lost me."

"Let me show you something." Cedric reached in his pocket and pulled out a small velvet box.

I held my hand to my chest and pointed. "Is that –" I watched as Cedric flipped the top of the box open to show a diamond.

I clapped my hands together and then lifted my arms in the air. "Praise the Lord! Cedric, that's beautiful. Carmen is going to love it. So when are you going to pop the question?"

He snapped the box closed. "Soon. I just need the right time. I'm glad you're happy, but I'm not sure what Carmen's answer will be."

"Of course, she's going to say yes. Why wouldn't she?"

"I always thought I would marry her. To be honest, the

moment I met her it was the first time marriage entered my mind. It's like we were meant to be."

"But..."

"I don't know if she's ready. I mean, I don't want to pop the question and get that silence or even a flat out no?"

"What would give you the impression that Carmen would consider saying no?"

"She's been pre-occupied for a while now. Carmen has been on a quest to search for her biological parents, which I totally support. I was hoping when we moved in together we could search together, but her friend Jocelyn has taken center stage now."

"You sound like you're not that fond of Jocelyn."

Cedric shook his head. "No, I wouldn't say that. Carmen is really close to her. They are really like sisters in a lot of ways. It's just that, I get that impression that Jocelyn has not always been a good influence on Carmen."

"Oh, I have met Jocelyn a couple of times. She seems like a sweet girl, well-intentioned like Carmen can be."

Cedric looked at me. "You don't know that much about Jocelyn's history, do you?"

For some reason, a vision of Detective Wilkes all-knowing look flashed in my mind. What was it she said?

People aren't always how they appear.

I closed my eyes. "Cedric, please don't tell me after thirty years of teaching, I have become that bad of a judge of character."

Cedric laughed. "Mama, calm down. I'm not saying Jocelyn is a murderer. Far from it, but according to Carmen, Jocelyn has been in trouble with the law. From my understanding it was petty theft and she was caught with marijuana when she was in high school."

"Mmm, I guess having a record made her more suspicious to the police. She's an adult now and seems settled in her job. I forgot what Jocelyn said she did for a living."

Cedric looked at me and shook his head. "You do know Jocelyn works at Hooters?"

"Hooters?"

Cedric turned a shade of red that I don't think I've seen before. "Please tell me you know what I'm talking about."

"Oh!" Then my mind started doing all kind of funny things. "Oh my word."

"Mama it's not that bad."

"No, no. Would you say that's the kind of place William would go?"

"William Hopkins? Probably."

I slapped my thigh. "Maybe that's where he saw Jocelyn."

Cedric frowned. "Why are you asking? You're not up to that snooping thing you were doing this past summer, right? I mean you're not planning to show up at Hooters?"

"Why? Have you been going there?"

Cedric answered back. "I haven't in a very long time."

"You and me both know that Carmen would whip your tail."

Cedric stood. "I agree. With that said, I'm going to head home now."

"You didn't stop at home first."

Cedric held out his arms. "You're still my number one girl, Mama."

With the kind of week I had, I so needed to hear that and I gladly accepted my hug. Who knows when I would get another one? Children become so stingy with affection the older they get.

As I watched Cedric walk down the porch steps, I thought about what he said about Jocelyn. I really did find sincerity in the young woman, but I wanted her to be more honest about her activity up until I found her by Louise's bedside last Sunday. Louise seemed at the center of all the mysteries of the last week, but Jocelyn was a catalyst.

I went back in the house and turned on my laptop. I noticed that Jocelyn had accepted my friend request on Facebook. Since I didn't have a phone number for her, I sent Jocelyn another message.

Jocelyn, we need to meet soon. I have so many questions and I truly want to help you, your mother and Louise connect.

Chapter 22

On Monday morning, I found a message from Jocelyn on Facebook. I thought it was a good sign that she wanted to talk to me too. After my conversation with Cedric and hearing his thoughts about Jocelyn, I felt like it was imperative that I talked to her again, maybe with a bit more of an open mind. Earlier this summer I let my guard down unknowingly with a person and missed catching significant clues about their character.

Jocelyn and I agreed to meet at my home around midmorning. Normally, Amos and I would have gotten together, but he was still on a secret mission. I noticed his truck was missing when I peeked out the living room window. I told myself I wasn't spying on Amos. Still, who stands by the window peeking out the blinds? Besides it was not any of my business what Amos did with his time. It would have been nice for Amos to finally meet Jocelyn in person and give me his expert opinion.

When the doorbell rang, I opened the door to find Jocelyn dressed in a navy sweatshirt, jeans and white sneakers. I thought she looked more subdued than the last two times we had met in person. She was at least twenty-six years old, but somehow she seemed so much younger. I opened the screen door. "Well, I was wondering if you knew how to get here. Come in."

Jocelyn didn't step inside right away, but looked over her left shoulder to Louise's house. She turned to me looking sheepish. "I've been in the neighborhood before."

I eyed Jocelyn. Now that didn't occur to me. "I imagine you've been searching around for Louise for some time, haven't you?"

Jocelyn nodded. "She'd been in that house for so many years. It seemed like a good place to start."

"That's a good point. Did you ever run across William while you were here in the neighborhood?"

"No, not here." Jocelyn looked down at the porch floor as though something was more interesting to her.

She didn't really answer my question. "Why don't you come inside? It's a bit chilly out there this morning."

Jocelyn stepped inside and I closed the door behind her. I had purposely left Porgy out to examine the guest. I have learned to monitor the dog and how he reacted to people. His comfort around my family and Amos spoke to his behavior and doggy thoughts of people. He sniffed around Jocelyn, but he didn't bark at her.

Jocelyn didn't seem to mind. She reached down and scratched Porgy behind the ears. "Such a cute dog."

"He's a good little watch dog. I inherited him this past summer."

Jocelyn smiled. "I miss having a pet. My family always had a dog." She looked around the living room. "You have a beautiful home, Ms. Eugeena."

I don't know why, but Jocelyn seemed nervous.

"Thank you. I have some questions, so I appreciate you stopping by so we can talk."

Jocelyn bit her lip. "I knew you probably had more questions after we talked over at Carmen's last week. I thought it might be best for you to talk to other members of my family."

"Your mother?"

"No, no. My aunts. Most of the information I have and that my mom knew came from my aunts Thelma and Ruth."

"I would love to meet them. When would be a good time?"

"Now. That's if you can come."

"Honey, I'm retired. I'm can come and go as I please. Let me get Porgy settled, and I will be ready to meet your aunts."

About ten minutes later, I climbed into Jocelyn's car. As she drove off, I hoped to get Jocelyn to talk more about herself. I really hadn't learned much about her. "I don't know why at my age I'm surprised by such a small world, but that's nice you have a friend like Carmen."

"Carmen is the closest person I have to a sister. One of the few people who has stuck by me through thick and thin."

"Jocelyn, you didn't tell me where you worked?"

Jocelyn kept her eyes on the road, but her skin grew reddish around the ears similar to my son's when he was embarrassed. "I haven't been as successful as Carmen. We both took the same college-level classes and I went to College of Charleston for a while."

I commented, "Well, life happens. We all sometimes end up on a path we don't plan."

"I strayed off my path because I got caught up with the

wrong guy. Carmen was always good about not dating and hanging out. She stuck to her studies. I guess that's why she's a physician now. I, on the other hand, got pregnant, dumped by the guy I thought loved me, lost the baby, and somewhere I lost myself. My mom wanted me to go back to school, but I have just worked different jobs over the years, mostly retail and waitressing."

"It's understandable. My daughter has had some difficulties after losing her best friend in a tragic accident. She's just now finding her way." I asked, "Is that what you do now? Waitressing?"

Jocelyn glanced at me. "I get decent tips. I have been saving to go back to school."

"Good for you! I was asking because the detective seemed to be concerned about William recognizing you somewhere. I just thought maybe he saw you at work."

Jocelyn was quiet for a moment "I have seen William Hopkins before last Sunday, but I didn't know who he was at the time. I just thought of him as an obnoxious customer."

"You served him at your job?"

"Yes, I did. He was there with some young guy. They always seemed to be talking business and I think I overhead something about some healthcare app. Sounded interesting."

"How many times do you think you've seen William?"

Jocelyn shrugged, "Hard to count. Maybe about three or four times?"

"He must have really liked the food at the restaurant."

Jocelyn glanced at me. "I'm sure there were other aspects that he liked. I work at Hooters. It's known for very pretty waitresses who don't mind showing..."

"I think I know."

"You can see why my mother stays disappointed in me. I don't even know if it was worth it to try to find my grand-mother."

"Why would your mother be so angry? It made sense to try again. It helps you know your own roots."

Jocelyn was quiet again before responding. "I think my mother blames Louise, you know, for my grandfather's death."

Why blame Louise? I wanted to say more, but decided to hold my tongue. It sounded to me like Louise and August naively fell in love at a time when it was not acceptable to be an interracial couple. They both were so young and I knew from personal experience becoming pregnant as a teenager wasn't the ideal time to enter motherhood.

We soon arrived at the Manning sisters' home. They lived in a neighborhood similar to Sugar Creek. As Jocelyn slowed down in front of a brick house, I heard her take in a sharp breath. "Oh no. She's not supposed to be here."

I leaned forward. "Who?"

Jocelyn pulled into the driveway behind a white Mer-cedes. She cut off the engine and sat staring ahead.

"Jocelyn, is this still a good idea to visit?"

She turned to me. "I don't know, it maybe your lucky day, Ms. Eugeena. You will get to meet my grandfather's sisters and my mother." With that Jocelyn opened the dri-ver's side and stepped out, her face full of anxiety.

I opened the passenger door, feeling a bit nervous. I was about to meet Louise's long lost daughter in the flesh. *How is Clarice Miller feeling about her biological mom now? Would she ever want to meet her?* She was Louise's only living child.

Chapter 23

I was reminded of Aunt Esther and Cora's home when we walked into the Manning house. The furniture wasn't old or shabby, or modern, but well cared for over the years. While the sisters didn't continue a public memorial, the seventeen years August Manning had lived were memorialized in many places in the living room. The same photo that Aunt Esther gave me hung larger than life above a fireplace.

I followed Jocelyn through the living room to where three women sat at a dining room table. They were laughing and enjoying what appeared to be a coffee cake. The women stopped talking and looked towards us. It was my first time seeing August's sisters. I could tell both were very pretty women when they were younger. Both in their seventies, they were very beautiful, sharing the same rich dark chocolate complexion as their deceased younger brother. Their large brown eyes and smile were warm and kind. I looked from them to the woman I really wanted to see up close.

Clarice Miller looked even more like Louise today. Her

eyebrow was raised in that same way Louise's eyebrow would arch when she inquisitive. I also noticed how blue Clarice's eyes looked against her honey-colored skin. Her hair flowed down her back reminding me a bit of the actress Vanessa Williams. She was Louise's daughter with no doubts.

Jocelyn cleared her throat. "Mom, Aunt Ruth and Thelma, this is Ms. Eugeena. She's the lady I told you about. Her aunt was one of grandfather's teachers."

I wasn't sure what angle Jocelyn wanted to go with after that introduction, but I stepped forward and stretched out my hand to both sisters. "It's so nice to meet all of you."

Ruth didn't stand, but I gathered from the walking cane that leaned against the table, she had some difficulty. She looked over at me over glasses that sat perched on her nose. Her smile was kind. "Who was your aunt? If she taught August, we probably had her as a teacher too."

I answered, "Esther Gibson."

Thelma clapped her hands together, "I remember Ms. Gibson. She was one of August's favorite teachers."

Ruth looked at her sister. "Ours too. I think we both became teachers because of Ms. Gibson."

I smiled. "That's good to know Aunt Esther had that kind of influence. I just retired after thirty years as a social studies teacher, and I must say she inspired me too."

I glanced at Clarice who was looking at me with interest and giving her daughter questioning looks. Jocelyn was looking everywhere except her mother's face. This was going to be an awkward conversation and I wondered how I could get some of my questions answered with Clarice present.

Thelma stood. "Let me get some more coffee made for us. Have a seat, Eugeena."

"Thank you." I pulled out the dining room chair noticing the set was the kind of furniture you don't find anymore. The chair was sturdy and beautifully assembled cherry wood. I sat down next to Jocelyn who seemed to being avoiding her mother's stare by staring at the center of the table.

I smiled at Clarice. "What do you do? Are you a teacher too?"

Clarice looked at me. "No, I probably have the most boring job of us all. I'm an accountant."

"That's pretty important." I thought to myself Clarice was a woman of details. She probably didn't miss much. I did want to know what happened to make her so angry with Jocelyn, and why she wouldn't try to touch base with Louise again.

Thelma stepped back into the dining room with a pot that was steaming. "Here is some fresh coffee. There are some plates there if you want to help yourself to the coffee cake."

I answered, "Oh I better not. I have diabetes and it's been a struggle trying to stay away from sweets."

Ruth and Thelma looked at each other and giggled. Ruth reached over and patted my hand. "Honey, you can eat this cake. We know all about diabetes since both of us are diabetics. We used Splenda with this recipe."

"Oh, well, then I would love to try a piece." I reached for the knife and cut off some cake placing it on a paper plate. When I brought the fork to my mouth, I savored the flavor. "Mmm, this is so good. I'm going to have to get this recipe."

Thelma shook her head, "Glad you like it. Now what did you want to ask us about August?"

The room which was full of energy before seemed to have changed. I swallowed the last piece of cake in my mouth and looked over at Jocelyn. "Well, I was really interested in how August passed. It appears like no one has ever solved his case?"

Ruth shook her head, "No, they haven't and we are content in our spirits that we will probably never see justice."

I asked, "Why is that?"

Thelma shook her head. "People were afraid to tell the truth back then and now it's just been too long for anyone but us to care."

Out of curiosity I inquired, "Do you have any idea who was responsible?"

Thelma looked over at Ruth. The sisters seemed to talk intimately with their eyes. Thelma finally responded, "We talked to the police and told them the names of the boys we suspected."

"Aunt Esther mentioned Bill Hopkins and Chuck Nelson. Sounds like others in the community suspected this too. I'm having a hard time about Bill Hopkins."

"Why is that?" Clarice who had been silent finally spoke. Her voice was sharp and piercing.

I glanced over at Jocelyn who stared at her mother as if to quietly tell her to calm down.

It was probably time to let Clarice know why I was really here. I leaned forward. "Bill Hopkins was my neighbor for many years. I'm good friends with his wife."

Clarice's mouth opened, but no words came out. She seemed shaken. "What is this, Jocelyn? What's going on?"

Jocelyn rolled her eyes. "Mom, I came to talk Aunt

Ruth and Thelma. I didn't know you were going to be here."

Clarice stood from the table, "So you're talking to people who know Louise Hopkins behind my back."

I frowned. "Louise and Bill were good people."

Clarice leaned forward on the table with her arms as if to steady herself. "Louise married the man who could have been responsible for dad's death."

"From what I've heard, Chuck Nelson was more in love with Louise. Bill may not have had anything to do with August's death."

Thelma reached over to touch Clarice's hand. "Clarice, please sit down. There's no need to be upset."

Clarice sank into the chair as if some force pushed her down.

Thelma continued, "That's true. Chuck grew up with Louise. In fact, Thelma and I have always suspected it was Chuck who went after August. It wasn't the first time he threatened him or tried to fight with August. He had an ugly temper."

Thelma chimed in, "Though Bill seemed to follow what Chuck said, he wasn't around that day. We think he probably suspected what Chuck did and didn't come forward."

Clarice spat, "That made him an accomplice."

Jocelyn slapped the table. "Then everyone who knew what Chuck did was an accomplice. It sounds to me like the police knew, but they didn't move forward because the Nelsons had power here."

Ruth and Thelma both nodded in agreement with Jocelyn.

I hadn't realized the family who owned the car dealership had more stakes in Charleston. "Clarice, would you mind if I asked what happened the day you tried to see Louise?"

Clarice looked at Jocelyn. "Why are you telling strangers my business?"

Jocelyn snapped back. "It's not just your business. Louise Hopkins is my grandmother. I'm an adult. The same way you chose to have a relationship with Aunt Ruth and Thelma, I can reach out and find out more about her if I want to."

Ruth held up her hands. "Calm down, both of you. There's no need to have this type of anger. Clarice, when you went to see Louise you were angry that day."

Clarice looked in the other direction.

I suspected she was near tears as I saw Jocelyn wipe away wetness from her own face. I felt helpless, but drawn to this family drama playing out. Secrets had devastated these women, but I really admired the Manning sisters. In all these years, they harbored no bitterness and didn't want that to infect the next generations.

Clarice turned around and spoke. She looked directly at me as though she wanted to break down any perceptions I may have had about Bill. "Mr. Hopkins answered the door that day I came. I already knew who he was from talking to Ruth and Thelma. I had these thoughts of how could he and Louise be married if he had something to do with my father's death. After he opened the door, he just looked at me. He finally asked who I was and I just told him my name was Clarice Miller and I wanted to meet Louise. He told me that it wasn't a good time and that it would be too painful for her. He thought I would bring back the past and all those memories."

Ruth added, "The day that Clarice went to see Louise, it was the anniversary of August's death." Ruth looked over at Clarice. "I told Clarice when she returned that Louise really did love August. I felt like he was her first love and she probably was grieving him, not knowing that Bill was keeping her child from her."

I sighed, thinking about what Bill did. I commented, "Bill was very protective of Louise. He sheltered her from her own son, William, and all his craziness when he could. Bill probably died a year or two after you came to see Louise that first time. Why didn't you try again? I believe she would have loved to have met you."

Clarice stared at me. "You know her that well. Did you even know I existed before my daughter showed up?"

Clarice had a point. Even though Louise didn't share her secret with me, I knew some things about her that the women in this room didn't. "Here's what I know. Louise had a child she miscarried in her first marriage. It was a boy. She married Bill later and she had a boy. I know when I had my daughter, Louise talked at length about always wanting a daughter and she so wanted grandchildren. Those are the things I know about Louise."

Clarice wouldn't look at me.

I continued, "She just lost her son. It would be lovely for her if she could have that chance to be a part of your life and your family. I saw it in her eyes. August is still close in her mind all these years later."

Clarice stood. "I can't. I just can't. Because she never searched for me."

Ruth spoke up. "That's not true. She did want to find you. Years ago she came to see us."

Thelma nodded. "She sat right here at this table and told us how she missed August. She never forgot about the child she gave up. That's why when we met you, we sent you to see her."

Clarice looked torn. "I have to go. It was good to meet you, Ms. Eugeena."

My heart sank in despair as I watched Clarice leave. I was hoping that Clarice would say she would be in touch or she would at least consider reaching out to Louise.

Chapter 24

The first thing I noticed when Jocelyn dropped me off at my house was Amos was back. His truck was parked out front. Now, of course, I would never admit to missing him, but after being around Jocelyn, her aunts and Clarice, I needed a breath of fresh air.

Jocelyn turned and parked her car in my driveway. There wasn't much I could say. I felt for Jocelyn who I sensed wanted peace with her mother. I looked at Jocelyn, "Your mother will eventually come around. We will pray her desire to be connected to her biological mother will grow."

"I'm hoping she sees we need family. I'm glad we're connected to my grandfather's side of the family, but I want us to be connected to our grandmother too. It seems to me like we all need each other."

I thought at that moment that Jocelyn with her struggles and quirky clothes was a very wise woman. I didn't know her well, but felt proud of her. I patted Jocelyn on the hand. "We will keep in touch. I will work on getting us a meeting with Louise."

"Thank you, Ms. Eugeena."

When I stepped out of the car, I had an urge to walk over to Amos' house, but thought I would wait. I still wondered what he had been up to this past weekend.

I said to myself out loud, "Eugeena, you really need to mind your business." I started laughing before I reached my porch steps. "Yeah right." By the time I opened the door, I figured I would check on Porgy and let him walk out in the backyard and then stroll next door.

Porgy ran around the yard taking time to sniff everything in sight while I stood on the patio. I looked over to Louise's house thinking of the times we would talk across the fence. A conversation from the past made me smile. I was outside with Leesa who was around two years old and was running as fast as her little legs would carry her over the grass. Louise was looking over the fence and laughing, tears of joy illuminated her blue eyes. She had said, "Eugeena, you are so blessed to have a girl. I imagine girls are fun."

Yes, girls could be fun and also a lot of work.

After I finally rounded Porgy back inside, the doorbell rang. *Who could that be?*

I opened the door and couldn't help but smile. "Well, someone must have missed me."

Amos grinned. "It's good to see you, Eugeena."

"You've been busy."

"I have been very productive."

"I certainly would like to hear more."

"How about we talk over dinner?"

I opened my mouth and closed it. Now I have cooked many meals for Amos and on rare occasions he has cooked on the grill or fried fish for us, but this invitation sounded a bit different.

Amos ignored my speechlessness, probably grateful that I wasn't running my mouth. "Someone told me you have a birthday coming up this Wednesday. I know your family would be around so I'd like to take you out for a birthday dinner tonight. If that's okay with you?"

"Oh." I held my hand to my chest. "That's quite nice of you, but..."

"I have lots to tell you. I can guarantee you will be interested."

Well how can a girl say no to that? "Okay, what time do you want to go to dinner?"

"I will come back around six o'clock."

"Sounds good." After I closed the door, I looked at the clock, noticing it was four o'clock now. *Is this considered a date?* Regardless, I had two hours to figure out what to wear.

Porgy watched me as I banged open my closet door and spent the next thirty minutes pulling out twenty pieces of clothing. I felt like I'd regressed in age. Who was this giddy teenage acting woman, because I certainly didn't recognize her? I finally settled on a comfortable, but very elegant purple sweater dress. It was a classic and had been hidden in the closet for some time. I used to not like to wear it because it showed off my rolls. I know they have spandex for hiding those areas of the body, but if I was going out for a special dinner with Amos, I at least wanted to enjoy my food.

After showering and getting dressed, I wasted more time until I found the right earrings. It took me a whole fifteen minutes to decide between the pearl studs and the gold hoops. Hoops won. I thought the earrings sparkled rather nicely next to my cropped gray hair. Plus, like the dress, I hadn't worn them in a few years.

I had one last thing to decide on. I really wasn't a makeup girl, although I tried to add a little lipstick on Sundays. I rarely went anywhere that called for makeup so I didn't see the need.

Of course tonight was different. I whipped out a little mascara and then added the lipstick.

I put my hands on my hip. "Eugeena, girl, you not looking too bad at all for almost sixty. People are going to be saying sixty what?"

The doorbell rang taking me out of my rare diva moment. I peered at the clock. It was five minutes to six o'clock. Well, someone was a bit early.

I opened the door to find a bouquet of flowers above legs and feet. I inquired, "Amos?"

Amos peeked around the flowers. Now I was used to either seeing Amos in overalls during the week or a suit on Sunday, but he was wearing a pair of nice khaki slacks and an olive green sweater. Very Heathcliff Huxtable, but I liked.

He stared at me in a way that made me want to rethink my outfit. I wasn't sure if he liked it, but he appeared surprised.

I asked, "Is this outfit okay for where we're going?"

He showed off all his pearly whites. "Perfect." He extended his arms towards me. "These are your birthday flowers."

"Oh my. Well I need to put these in water before we head out." I was glad I hadn't put my heels on yet or I would have toppled over trying to balance the huge bouquet. I can't say I have ever seen an arrangement quite so colorful.

I walked into the kitchen and placed the flowers on the table and then reached under the cabinet to find a vase.

When I stood up, I was very aware that Amos must have walked in behind me. Feeling self-conscious I filled water in the vase and then walked over to the table. I smiled as I arranged the flowers in the vase. "These are really nice."

"Well, I hope you like where I made reservations for us tonight too."

"Reservations?" Amos went all out. I couldn't wipe the silly grin off my face if I tried. "Let's go. I just need to put my shoes on."

I stopped and grabbed my heels, thankful that they were a reasonable height.

After I locked the front door, I noticed Amos had opened the car's passenger door. This was certainly not the first time I'd rode in his car, but it felt like the first time of something.

We were quiet as Amos drove. I was really curious what restaurant Amos chose. I could see we were heading towards Charleston's waterfront. I asked, "Seafood?"

Amos looked over at me. "The best."

Five minutes later we pulled up in front of Fleet Landing. It was hard to believe the chic restaurant used to be a place for sailors back in World War II. Reservations were definitely highly recommended and I, until tonight, had never eaten there. "This is definitely a first."

Amos winked. "It's only going to get better."

While Amos parked the car, I was starting to feel warm. Not like I was running a fever, but excited that I was going to enjoy myself in a way I had not in a long time.

When we arrived, the hostess checked our reservations and showed us to our table. The scene outside the window was breathtakingly beautiful. I'd grown up in Charleston all my life, but I sometimes forgot how close I was to the Atlantic Ocean and how majestic it looked up close.

We took some time to order, but I finally decided I could not resist the blackened shrimp alongside the pimento cheese grits. *Why haven't I thought to try this before now?*

While we waited, I filled Amos in on my visit with August's sisters. "They seemed pretty convinced that Chuck Nelson was the culprit. His dad was pretty powerful and as you can see the Nelsons continue to have their businesses here in Charleston. It's just a shame that no one had enough evidence to charge him."

Amos nodded. "Well, people don't always get what we think they deserve, but God has a way of fixing that."

I leaned forward. "So, what have you been up to? You've been out of pocket since we left the dealership on Saturday."

Amos placed his elbows on the table. "That's because I decided to check out a few things."

"Well, don't keep me in suspense."

"I went to see Chuck Nelson."

I sucked in a breath. "You did?" Then I sat up straighter. "Without me?"

Amos chuckled. "I was going on a hunch. There was no need for both of us to be there. Besides that the man's been under your nose in a way. He's in the same place as Louise."

"Chuck Nelson is at Hillcrest Manor Nursing Home. You just walked in to see him? I haven't been able to see Louise in days."

"Nope, didn't have a problem at all. I wasn't sure when I went what I would find. I can tell you that ole Chuck is in the Alzheimer's unit. Probably last stages."

"How did you know he was there?"

"I did a little digging. I started at his house and his daughter answered the door. She told me that they had to put him in a nursing home. We kept talking and I found out it was Hillcrest. Like I said when I found him, he wasn't very communicative."

"So no confessions at this point?"

"I'm afraid not."

The waiter showed up at our table with the steaming plates of food. The pimento cheese and shrimp on the grits was just heavenly. I swallowed a few more bites before asking, "Did you try to see Louise while you were there?"

"I did, but you know the strangest thing was I was told that she wasn't able to see any visitors."

"Really? For a while there I was thinking it was just me. So let me get this straight, you were able to see Chuck Nelson, but not Louise?"

"That's right."

"How is that even possible?"

"That's what we need to figure out, which brings me to something else I ran across. There seems to be some other residents at Hillcrest Manor who can't have visitors who are not family or who are suddenly not included on the visitor's log. I talked to at least four people who said the person they were trying to visit has relatives who live far away or they were on their own."

I sucked in my breath. "That's doesn't seem right at all. It's almost like these people are being isolated on purpose. Isn't that elder abuse?"

Amos nodded. "Something isn't quite right. Oh, but you haven't heard the really big find."

"Tell me."

"It seems as though Hillcrest Manor is owned by

Chuck Nelson's family. In fact, one of the staff members told me the room where Chuck stays was designed exactly like his room at home. Staff is asked to keep an eye on him, but he's not to know or have any hints that he's not home."

"Seems to me like he should have even more privacy, and protection being an Alzheimer's patient. You know I always thought that place was nice, but it seems to be not what it appears to be."

Amos commented, "That's not uncommon in nursing homes, which is why I'm thinking it might be a good idea to bring in the Department of Social Services. Of course, someone to actually report evidence of anything out of the ordinary would be a better place to start. Any word from Pat?"

I shook my head. "No. It's been over three days now." What was that buzzing? "Hold on just a minute, Amos. You know every time Pat has called me on this thing I always miss her. I wonder who this could be calling me now."

I recognized the phone number, but my mind was a bit muddled so I didn't recognize who's number. I was getting better with technology, but I didn't always fill out my contacts like I should. I answered, "Hello."

"Eugeena, its Annie Mae. "

I looked at Amos. "Annie Mae, what's going on?"

"They found Pat."

"Is she okay?"

I almost dropped the phone as I heard the wail that came through. I lifted the phone back to my ear and looked over at Amos who was watching me with concern. "Hello, Annie Mae."

All I could hear was the sound of wailing in the background. A strained voice came back on the phone,

"Eugeena, she's gone. I don't understand how she could be gone."

Chapter 25

Amos was a real trooper. He paid the bill and drove us to the Browns. While I have had some difficulties getting along with Willie Mae and Annie Mae, I wouldn't have wished this kind of news on my worst enemy. I knew they were both devastated. We all had prayed together for many years and tried to intervene for Pat when she was going through heroin addiction. She fought so hard to get her life back on track.

I can't believe she is gone. I hope I misunderstood Annie Mae.

I was beside myself the whole way and was so thankful Amos was driving. I knew Pat had been trying to tell me something. Pat showed concern from the beginning about Louise's welfare and fussed at William hours before he was killed. For the past week and a half, what happened to poor William haunted me. Now Pat too.

That was two people who I'd watched grow up. We needed answers.

Annie Mae answered the door when we arrived. I don't think in all the years I had known her I'd ever hugged her. I felt slightly guilty that such a tragedy brought us to this moment, but a hug was more than appropriate. Annie Mae seemed too distraught to protest. I caught her looking at Amos behind me, but there were no judgmental remarks.

Grief overwhelmed me as I walked into the room and saw Willie Mae sitting with her arms crossed as if she was freezing cold. Pat was her only child. She glanced at me, but turned her attention to the person sitting across from her. I have to say I was a bit surprised to see Detective Wilkes there.

"Willie Mae, I'm so sorry to hear about Pat." I looked at the detective who eyed me and then Amos.

"You two again?" Detective Wilkes remarked.

I sighed, "Charleston is a good size city, Detective, but some of us have been here all our lives and know each other. We all go to the same church."

Detective Wilkes nodded. "I see."

Amos stepped up and asked the detective, "If you're here it sounds like something happened to Pat that could be considered foul play."

The petite detective peered at Willie Mae. "Unfortunately, we can't say that at this time, but Ms. Brown's death needs further investigation. We have requested an autopsy."

Willie Mae shook her head. "They're trying to say she overdosed."

"No," I said. "That can't be."

Detective Wilkes responded, "It's my understanding that in the past Ms. Brown had been addicted to heroin."

Willie Mae threw her hands up in the air. "She beat her addiction. That was years ago. She wouldn't go back to that stuff again."

Detective Wilkes looked down at her notebook as if this pained her to ask. "Was Ms. Brown under any stress or were there any changes that may have motivated her to consider using drugs again?"

Willie Mae's voice cracked with frustration. "She wouldn't go touch that stuff again." She began to sob softly into her hands.

Annie Mae came up beside her sister on the couch and put her arm around her twin. "Please leave. We need time to grieve."

Detective Wilkes stood. "I will be in touch when we have any other information. Ladies, I'm truly sorry for your loss."

I grabbed Amos' arm and pulled him after the detective. Once we were outside, I asked the detective. "Can we talk?"

Detective Wilkes turned around. "If you have something that can help."

I took a deep breath. "Something has been different about the nursing home where Pat worked."

Detective Wilkes looked at me. "So, you agree that Ms. Brown was stressed... that she could have regressed."

"It's a possibility, but I don't think so. Pat had developed a solid faith in the past few years. She cared about her patients, loved her Sunday School class and belted out the most beautiful solos on Sunday morning; I can't believe she would want to go back to that place of misery. She was trapped there for so many years."

I felt Amos' hand on my shoulder. I hadn't realized tears were streaming down my face. I wiped them away with the end of my sleeve.

This was my theory. "I think Pat was harmed. She has been trying to get in touch with me all last week, but we kept missing each other. Whatever she wanted to tell me, she certainly didn't feel comfortable just telling me over the phone. She kept insisting on meeting in person."

Detective Wilkes looked thoughtful for a minute.

Amos nudged the detective. "Detective Wilkes, was there more to Pat's condition other than she appeared to have overdosed?"

"I can't really say, Mr. Jones. I will say that there's always the possibility that someone could have helped her along. The medical examiner noticed something, but I'm not at liberty to say." The detective looked at us. "Looks like you two were out having a good time. Sorry this messed up your evening."

I looked down at the dress I was wearing. A sudden gust of wind reminded me how cold the world could be. I'd forgotten that Amos and I had been enjoying a dinner out. I guess one would have called it a date. All that excitement I had earlier had dissipated.

It was almost ten o'clock when we arrived back home. When Amos pulled into my driveway, I said, "Thank you for the evening you had planned for us."

"Sorry about Pat. This is mind boggling. I've looked over many cases in my life, but this has me wondering what's going on."

I turned to Amos. "Do you agree we should find out?"

"Eugeena, I would have to agree with you, but I don't know what we can do."

"How about trying to see Louise?"

"It's a start. We can't be rash. They do have some type of security."

I understood what Amos was saying, but I knew I could no longer stay in the dark about what was going on with my friend. I was feeling too insecure about her being in *that* place.

Chapter 26

I didn't sleep, but I talked to God. I asked why several times in between getting caught up in my own tears. By the time I awakened, I was determined to get my answers. It occurred to me I was more distraught over Pat's death than William's death. Both deaths were sudden and tragic. There were too many questions left hanging. I wasn't sure if one was connected to the other, but I couldn't get bogged down in details. The goal was to see how Louise was doing.

After I parked in the Hillcrest Manor Nursing Home parking lot, I marched inside and to my surprise no one was at the desk. I just knew Lexi would be there with her condescending little face telling me I was not allowed to visit Louise.

I thought why not just sneak down the hallway. A big and hulky male was pushing a man in a wheelchair past me. Maybe I will just go back to my original plan, which was to confront the director. She was the one making the rules and she argued with Pat about something last week that upset Pat. So I switched direction down another hall-way towards the administration offices.

I moved through a sitting area that I hadn't been in before towards a few doors. All the doors were closed, but the lights were on from what I could tell from the window panes next to the doors. As I approached the door in the far corner of the administration area, I read the gold name-plate. Jacqueline Saunders, Director. That's who I needed to see first.

I started to knock on the door, but I could hear voices. It sounded like a man and a woman were arguing. I looked at the table in the middle of the sitting area; I went over and grabbed a brochure off of the table. I scoped the nearby doors to see if there was anyone who could see me and eased as close as I could to Ms. Saunders's door. If the door opened, I could always say I was waiting to see her.

I leaned towards the door close enough hoping that I didn't look like I was eavesdropping. It was so hard to hear.

I heard the man's voice yell, "What were you doing with my car?"

Ms. Saunders raised her voice, "I told you I just needed to borrow your car because mine was in the shop."

"So you just came in my house and took the keys. That's technically stealing. I don't care if you are family, especially with some detective showing up asking me questions. Do you know how embarrassing that is to have customers see policemen walking through the show-room?"

Showroom? Like a car showroom. Wait a minute, I know that voice.

That was James Nelson. Amos said the nursing home was owned by the Nelsons. It made sense for James to come visit his father, Chuck Nelson. How would Jacqueline Saunders be able to borrow his car? What kind of car was it?

Jacqueline asked, "What were they asking you?"

I strained to hear.

"The detective was asking me about William. Seems like my car could have been at his house the night he was shot."

Jaqueline responded matter-of-factly. "I'm sure there are a lot of other cars like your Mustang here in Charleston. Now what did you tell them about the car?"

"Can I help you?"

I shrank back and noticed a red-haired woman was looking at me strangely. I smiled and held out the brochure. "I was waiting to talk to Ms. Saunders."

The woman pointed to the sitting area. "Looks like she is with someone now, why don't you have a seat?"

After what I just heard, I had a change of plan. "You know what? I will be back."

I hurried out of the area and fast as I could. I looked over at the front desk again. Lexi was still not there. I stopped and pulled out my phone. I told Amos I was coming to the nursing home and would call him if I found anything strange.

Amos answered on the first ring. "Everything okay, Eugeena? Have you seen Louise yet?"

I looked around to make sure no one was listening to my conversation. "That's next, but I need you to know that I overheard a conversation. You know that car that was at the house the night William was killed?"

"Yes."

"It could belong to James Nelson. But get this; Jacqueline Saunders could have been driving it. How?"

Amos was quiet for a moment like he was thinking.

"According to the information I found, the former director was Jacqueline's mother. She retired and passed the nursing home to her daughter. It's possible James Nelson and Jacqueline Saunders are related, maybe even siblings."

That's the connection! I turned and saw someone coming down the hallway. I walked over to the other side of the hallway and held my head down. It appeared to be James Nelson. I recognized the salesman's determined strides as he pushed open the door. "Amos, I'm going to see if I can get down the hallway to Louise while I still have a chance. I made need a little backup."

"What are you planning to do?"

"Let's just say I'd like to get a conversation going with Ms. Saunders, but I know I need some help."

"Eugeena?"

"You told me to call you when I'm about to get into something? I'm letting you know now." I clicked off the conversation before Amos tried to talk me out of whatever sketchy plan I had in my head.

Then I scooted down the hallway. I had visions of me being dressed as a nurse, but that was taking it a bit too far. *No need for a disguise.* I passed the sitting area for residents and noticed some of the same people sitting around watching the television. No one seemed to notice me walking past. The closer I got to Louise's room I was feeling hopeful that this would all work out fine.

Right outside Louise's room, I heard someone talking to Louise in a harsh voice. "Pat is off today. Now you need to take your medicine."

Louise whined. "Where's Pat? I want Pat. She knows I don't need to take this stuff. I don't want it. It doesn't make me feel good."

I hoped Amos was coming with the cavalry because I was putting a stop to this foolishness, right then.

Chapter 27

I stepped in the room to see Lexi with a syringe in her hand. "So you're the receptionist and the nurse. Honey, you got some explaining to do because I don't think you're qualified to be giving anybody what's in that needle."

"Eugeena, thank goodness you're here. I really want to go home, but no one will take me."

Lexi frowned. "What are you doing here? You're not supposed to be in here."

"Well, why don't you get Ms. Saunders? Louise and I have to have a talk with her."

Lexi looked unsure and I was not happy with her holding up that syringe. I took my phone out. "I will call social services if you don't put that syringe down. I see something that looks suspiciously like elder abuse to me."

Louise rose up in the bed. "That's exactly what it is, Eugeena. You get her."

Lexi looked at Louise like she was going to stick her with the syringe anyway, but she moved past me. She threatened, "I will be back."

I turned towards Louise and watched as she blinked

back tears, "I don't like her. She's not very nice. Something has happened to Pat. I haven't seen her in days."

This wasn't the time to upset Louise. "I know your favorite nurse is Pat. Now, how are you doing?"

Louise pointed to a notebook by her side. "I have William's funeral planned out. It's been hard to do because I seem to sleep all the time."

I smiled and reached for the notebook. "I'm sorry I haven't been here for you. You should have had someone here to help you."

"Have they found out anything about my William?"

"Not that I know of. Did you two get a chance to talk on Sunday?"

"A little. I kind of wasn't listening to him. I had other things on my mind."

"You know he had someone buying the house."

Louise tilted her head. "Yes, I remember him saying there was a buyer. I hope they would change their mind and not want the house. That's my house, Eugeena."

"Mrs. Patterson, you need to leave the premises."

I looked up to see Ms. Saunders at the door. The large male nurse I had seen earlier was behind her.

I started to protest, but Louise changed my mind.

"Jacqueline, why would you ask Eugeena to leave? She's my friend."

Jacqueline stepped in the room as if she was coming to remove me herself.

Louise kept talking. "Eugeena, did you know William has been in love with this woman since they were teenagers?"

"No, I didn't. I would love to hear more about this."

Jacqueline froze looking from Louise to me.

"Oh yes, during high school William was so in love

with her. They went to the senior prom together. I still have that photo somewhere, not sure where it is now."

I decided to help Louise speed up these revelations. "So do you think William still had a thing for Ms. Saunders?"

"Oh yes, that's why he was all cleaned up last week. I think they have been going out together."

"No!" Ms. Saunders shouted. "You're wrong. There was nothing going on between William and me."

I thought back to Sunday.

It's just the way I remember it. That strange comment from the female buyer of the house made sense now. Jacqueline knew that house. "So, Jacqueline, you must have spent a lot of time at the Hopkins house. Louise, did you know that Jacqueline loved your house so much she wanted to buy it?"

Louise looked at Jacqueline. "You? Why would you buy my house?"

"A better question is why did she shoot William?"

Jacqueline turned a shade of red that I wanted to say looked dangerously close to purple. "I did no such thing."

"But your brother, James Nelson, just said you borrowed his car. That would be a Mustang, right? The police were just asking him about the car. He must be real upset with you that you took his car and used it as a getaway car."

Jacqueline roared, "I knew I should have taken care of you. You just don't quit. All of your questions."

"Like Pat. Who probably didn't really quit either?"

With that Jacquelyn turned around and fled the room. She pushed past the big male nurse who was standing behind her.

I yelled at him. "What kind of nurse are you? Protect your patients. That woman is a murderer. Go get her."

The man looked at me like he was crazy but took off down the hallway.

Louise looked bewildered, "What just happened?"

"We just called out a killer?" My phone rang and I saw it was Amos. I answered the phone and yelled, "She's getting away. What should we do?"

Amos responded, "No, she's not. We got her."

I smacked myself on the head. "You did! That was fast."

"Detective Wilkes was already on it. Apparently, she'd asked James Nelson to wear a wire when he was talking with his sister earlier." When he left, that was the cue for the police to enter the nursing home.

I inhaled deeply and then blew out a breath, feeling tension leaving my body. "That worked out pretty good. I managed not to get into too much trouble."

"I told you to let God handle it."

I laughed, but I still wanted answers. What exactly was Jacqueline Saunders trying to hide that cost William and Pat their lives?

Chapter 28

It seemed like hours went by before anyone came back to let Louise and I know what was going on. We took the time to catch up as best we could. I asked, "Louise, do you remember the young woman who came to visit last Sunday? Did you understand who she was?"

Louise smiled. "Not really, but she reminded me of a person I knew a long time ago."

There was my cue. "August?"

Louise looked startled.

"I've learned a lot about you, my dear friend. You want to tell me more about him."

Louise grinned. "I see you have been busy. I have always wanted to tell you about him. It just never was the right time. August Manning was one of my dearest friends from the time I was a little girl. It was hard for us to be friends the older we got. People warned us to be careful, but we were young and in love."

"You said it never was the right time to tell me about him. Why? Did you feel uncomfortable bringing him up especially around Bill, maybe?"

"Bill and I never talked about August, but he knew when the anniversary of his death came around that I needed alone time. I know there were rumors."

"So you knew the rumors about Chuck Nelson."

"I confronted him."

"You did? Well, what did he say?"

"He denied it, but I knew it was him. It was Chuck who told my parents that I was pregnant. A few days later I got shipped off to this home. It was terrible there. They wouldn't let me see the baby. I kind of felt like the baby was a girl. I can't explain it. But I have always been haunted by her cries and knowing how August died and that no one would listen to me. I had a baby out of wedlock with a black man. I thought years later when I lost my other baby that is was punishment."

"Oh Louise. No."

"I know better now. Eugeena, do you think I will ever meet her? That was my daughter in that photo."

"I'm pretty sure you will see your granddaughter again. Her name is Jocelyn. We will work on Clarice."

"That's her name? Clarice."

"Yes."

"That was my grandmother's name."

Amos showed up at the door of Louise's room.

Louise shouted, "Amos, my friend, it is so good to see you. I feel like I've been rescued." Louise's shoulders sank. "I just don't know what I've been rescued from."

Amos chuckled. "I will do my best to fill you ladies in, just know that my old detective brain is still trying to process all that I've seen in the last hour."

Amos pulled over a chair from under the television next to the bed. After he sat down and caught his breath.

"Well, for the news you're probably waiting for, Jacqueline Saunders is in police custody."

I said, "That was fast. Did you call them after we got off the phone?"

Amos nodded. "I did call Detective Wilkes, but she informed me they already had everything under control. When you saw James Nelson here earlier, he was in her office with a wire."

"He was setting his sister up?"

"That's right. James might be a slick car salesperson, but he's a good man. According to the detective, James had been suspicious about his sister's return to town for months. He was friends with William and didn't think his sister was being sincere with her intentions.

Louise looked confused, "William didn't mention he'd been seeing Jacqueline. Of course, he didn't talk to me. He was so in love with her. She broke his heart years ago."

Amos said, "It seems like William and Jacqueline were caught up with a group of people working on several scams at the same time. I can't get into all of them, but that healthcare app startup company was one of them. They had a lot of investors, but no one was seeing the product come through in a timely fashion."

I nudged Amos. "What about here at the nursing home? What was going on?"

Amos sighed. "Yeah, well, there have been some suspicions here for a while even before Jacqueline started as the new director. It seems that Jacqueline and her staff that she brought on had been quietly doing some false Medicare claims. Pat may have caught on to some of this when she started to see nurses being let go."

I asked, "And by staff did that include that Lexi woman? She was young, pixie haircut. I always thought there some something strange about the chick. I caught her trying to give Louise a syringe full of something."

Louise's eyes widened. "I never thought she was a nurse, but what do I know?"

Amos nodded. "I think she was one of the ones in handcuffs out there. There were at least three women. One was the accountant and I believe she had red hair. Anyhow, there seemed to be an even bigger issue and here is where I think William and Jacqueline might have clashed. The detective will have to let you know more, but Jacqueline had power of attorney over her dad the same as William had power of attorney over your estate, Louise."

Louise shook her head. "I don't even remember signing anything. I kept telling him I was fine. I have been taking care of myself. So what were they doing with the money?"

I shouted, "Stealing. They were stealing money from their own parents. I still don't know why Jacqueline shot William. I can see Pat catching her in the act of filing wrongful Medicare claims."

Amos nodded. "It's just a theory now, because Detective Wilkes wouldn't let me hear too many details, but I think William started to get the sense that Jacqueline was trying to cut everyone out of their slice of money. He may have asked her about a discrepancy in a bill from the nursing home, and well, things escalated from there."

Louise rubbed her arms. "That girl always had a temper like her dad, Chuck."

"Mrs. Hopkins?"

We all turned towards the door to see the large male nurse.

Amos grinned. "Good work, Agent Skinner."

I raised an eyebrow at the large man. "Agent? You look like a nurse to me."

Agent Skinner walked into the room. "Undercover. Hello, you must be Ms. Eugeena. I heard a lot about you today."

I blinked. "Really? Who exactly are you an agent with?

"FBI, ma'am. I must say you pulled together details of the case rather well in a few days."

"Oh, well, thank you. I had some help. So you've been looking at this place for a while now?"

"A few months. Just so happens our sting operation was planned for today. Unfortunately, we're sorry we lost Pat Brown. She was a good source."

Louise looked confused. "No one has told me what happened to Pat."

I tried to figure out what was the best way to tell Louise, but someone else was at the door. I sucked in a breath and found my eyes watering at the sight.

Jocelyn stepped in the room. "Is it okay if we come in? We saw the news, and wanted to check in on Ms. Louise. It looks you have lot of visitors today."

I peered at Jocelyn. "Sure, you both can come in."

Jocelyn turned towards the door. "Mom?"

Clarice took a tentative step inside the room.

I grabbed Amos' arm and squeezed.

He leaned over. "Is that...?"

"Yes. Agent Skinner, why don't we let these ladies have the room? I would love to hear more about Pat's involvement in the case."

As we all squeezed out of the room, I turned to see Louise clutching her hands as she looked at Clarice and Jocelyn. As I thought it would happen, Jocelyn made the first move and hugged Louise. She turned and waved her mom over.

I sniffled because I was so happy for Louise, but I was so sad about Pat. Willie Mae and Annie Mae lost a daughter. Louise found hers.

It was all pretty bittersweet.

Epilogue

It took a few weeks to recuperate after all that crazy business at Hillcrest Manor. All of it was over now. I was just happy to be surrounded by family. I don't think I'd ever had this many people in my dining room for Thanksgiving dinner. Junior arrived with his crew early Thursday morning. Cedric and Carmen arrived soon after. It helped moved things along in the kitchen much better with Carmen and Leesa.

After everyone had finished eating, I started to clear off the table. When I walked back into the kitchen I took a big sigh of relief. I turned on the faucet and placed my hand under the water to test the temperature. Once I was satisfied, I plugged the drain hole and added some liquid detergent. I could have used the dishwasher, but I kind of wanted the reflection time.

Dinner was a success, though there were a few awkward moments at the table which mainly consisted of all of my children scolding me about my latest snooping. Thankfully, Amos defended me, promising he wouldn't let me get into any trouble. It still made me wonder how much talking went on behind my back in particularly with my sons.

The highlight was definitely seeing that beautiful sparkling diamond on Carmen's hands. I knew better than to ask when the wedding was. I was still hoping Leesa was taking things slow although it was good to see Chris and Leesa together. I hugged Chris and thanked him for coming. I guess he wasn't too bad, but only time would tell.

I turned around from the sink to see Louise shuffling in the kitchen with her hands full of dishes. Behind her was Jocelyn. It was really lovely to see how Louise and Jocelyn had connected. It reminded me of the first time I saw them together at the nursing home. All the emotion of the moment.

So much had happened since then.

"Thank you, ladies. Just set the dishes on the counter. Now, you are both guests. You really should relax."

Louise placed plates on the counter and turned to me with her nose scrunched. "A guest? Oh Eugeena, I'm so happy to be in *my* home and I'm getting to know my beautiful girl here. Did you tell Eugeena your news?"

Jocelyn smiled. "I was accepted into the nursing program. I will start in January."

I reached over to hug Jocelyn. "Oh I'm so happy for you."

"I have Ms. Pat to thank. She gave me the idea and told me how she went back to school after she finished at rehab."

That sounded like Pat. Lord knows that girl has been missed.

"Grams, I'm going to head out. Mom is over with August's sisters."

Louise nodded. "Yes, Clarice told me she would be there today. I plan to visit with them over Christmas."

Jocelyn tilted her head. "You two are talking more regularly. That's a good sign."

"Yes, it is. Let's have a hug. We don't want to hold you up."

Jocelyn hugged Louise and then me.

After she left, I placed the dishes in the sink and then asked, "How are you really doing, Louise?"

Louise's eyes were shining. "I'm blessed. I miss William even though he didn't come around much for the holidays; it feels different that he won't ever be around."

"He's with you in spirit. I believe in his own way, he wanted to protect you."

Louise's blue eyes were vibrant, but sad tears spilled down her cheeks. She swallowed. "Me too. It's a lot to digest sometimes. My...daughter. We have a lot of catching up to do. She's so beautiful. August would have been proud."

I squeezed Louise's hands. "I know Jocelyn has already taken a liking to you. How does it feel to have a granddaughter?"

"It's good. I'm so glad she's going back to school. It's never too late to make something of yourself."

"No, it's not."

Louise smiled. "Never too late for other things too."

I eyed her. "Louise?"

Louise rubbed her tummy. "Amos did an excellent job of frying that turkey. I wonder what else you would let him do."

"Okay, time for you to exit my kitchen, Louise Hopkins. I don't want to know what you're thinking."

She reached out and grabbed my hand. "You know I lost my very first love, the second one was a bust, but Bill was my heart for fifty years. What I'm trying to say is I believe God gives us many chances at love. Don't you agree?"

I didn't have a chance to answer because Amos walked in with an armful of plates.

"Oh my goodness. I told you people to relax and enjoy yourself." I took a pan from Amos and sat it on the counter. From the side I watched Louise scatter from the room. I shook my head, but then a case of nervousness came over me. I almost dropped a bowl, but Amos reached out and caught it before it hit the floor.

"What would I do without you?" I asked, playfully.

Amos smiled, "I was kind of hoping you'd realize I'm here to support you. So what do you need me to do – wash or dry?"

"I think washing would do fine." It gave me a chance to dry the dishes and admire the man I knew I was starting to love.

About the Author

Tyora Moody is the author Soul-Searching Suspense novels in the Serena Manchester Series, Victory Gospel Series and the Eugeena Patterson Mysteries. As a literary-focused entrepreneur, she has assisted countless authors with developing an online presence via her design and marketing company, Tywebbin Creations LLC. Popular services include virtual event planning, social media management, book trailers and book covers. She is also the author of the nonfiction series, *The Literary Entrepreneur's Toolkit*, and the host of *The Literary Entrepreneur Podcast*.

Tyora won 2nd Place for the 2014 Yerby Award for Fiction. She is the 2013 Urban Literary Awards Debut Author Winner and 2013 Urban Literary Awards Mystery / Thriller / Suspense Winner. Tyora is a member of Sisters in Crime and American Christian Fiction Writers. For more information about her literary endeavors, visit her online at TyoraMoody.com

CPSIA information can be obtained
at www.ICGtesting.com
Printed in the USA
LVHW020445290422
717484LV00010B/927